LOVE INSPIRED SUSPENSE
INSPIRATIONAL ROMANCE

Colorado Ambush

AMITY STEFFEN

D0060494

LOVE INSPIRED SUSPENSE
INSPIRATIONAL ROMANCE

Courage. Danger. Faith.

Find strength and determination in stories of faith and love in the face of danger.

AVAILABLE THIS MONTH

SEARCH AND DEFEND
HEATHER WOODHAVEN

TEXAS RANCH REFUGE
LIZ SHOAF

ROCKY MOUNTAIN STANDOFF
LAURA SCOTT

COLORADO AMBUSH
AMITY STEFFEN

WILDERNESS HIDEOUT
HOPE WHITE

BURIED COLD CASE SECRETS
SAMI A. ABRAMS

ISBN-13: 978-1-335-55477-2

9 781335 554772

50599

EAN

A woman and a girl were hopping into his boat. The woman gave the starter rope a powerful tug.

"Hey!" He strode across the grass, waving an arm at them. "That's my boat!" he shouted.

The woman ignored him, even as the young girl stared at him in what looked like fear.

When it became clear that she didn't care that the boat was his, he took off running.

"Hey, you! Stop!" he tried again.

The girl unlashed the rope that held the boat to the dock. With another yank, the woman managed to get his cantankerous motor to chug to life. The boat spurted forward.

Jesse launched himself off the dock. His feet landed with a solid thud. "What do you think you're doing?" he demanded. "Didn't you hear me? This is my boat."

"Get down!" The woman made the command, but not to him. He twisted in time to see the child duck, and he was shocked by what he spotted on the shore. Two gunmen were taking aim at them.

Amity Steffen lives in northern Minnesota with her two boys and two spoiled cats. She's a voracious reader and a novice baker. She enjoys watching her sons play baseball in the summer and would rather stay indoors in the winter. She's worked in the education field for more years than she cares to count, but writing has always been her passion. Amity loves connecting with readers, so please visit her at Facebook.com/amitysteffenauthor.

Books by Amity Steffen

Love Inspired Suspense

Reunion on the Run
Colorado Ambush

COLORADO AMBUSH

AMITY STEFFEN

LOVE INSPIRED SUSPENSE
INSPIRATIONAL ROMANCE

LOVE INSPIRED® SUSPENSE
INSPIRATIONAL ROMANCE

ISBN-13: 978-1-335-55477-2

Colorado Ambush

Copyright © 2021 by Amity Steffen

PLEASE RECYCLE
THIS PRODUCT IS RECYCLABLE

Recycling programs
for this product may
not exist in your area.

This edition published by arrangement with Harlequin Books S.A.

For questions and comments about the quality of this book, please contact us
at CustomerService@Harlequin.com.

Love Inspired
22 Adelaide St. West, 40th Floor
Toronto, Ontario M5H 4E3, Canada
www.LoveInspired.com

Printed in U.S.A.

For I, saith the Lord, will be unto her a wall of fire round about, and will be the glory in the midst of her.
—*Zechariah* 2:5

For my parents,
whose support over the years means the world to me.

ONE

The small motorboat rocked under Jesse McGrath's weight as he stepped aboard. He set his fishing rod down and dropped onto the bench seat near the motor. It was a beautiful spring day, perfect to get some fishing in. As long as he stayed in the bay and out of the wind.

He let out a growl of frustration when he realized he must've left his life jacket in the fish-cleaning shack the night before. Colorado's regulations stated he needed one in the boat. Far be it from him to break the law.

He must've left his life jacket hanging on the hook inside the door after he cleaned up his catch for dinner last night. He clambered to his feet, hopped back out onto the dock and headed toward the small pine-sided building that was set back from the shoreline.

The red life jacket was hanging inside, on a hook to the right of the door, just as he'd assumed. The unexpected sound of a whispered voice—a panicked voice—caught his attention. The hurried tread of footsteps scampering across the ground set his instincts on high alert.

Jesse slid his hand to where his holstered gun usually rested. Of course, it wasn't there. He was on vacation, taking some time off from his job as a deputy with the Cascade Falls Sheriff's Department. He'd told his supervisor it was only temporary, but after a week of rumination, he wasn't so sure. Maybe the life of a law enforcement officer wasn't for him anymore.

Thankfully, he didn't need to make that decision right now. *Now* he was going to get some fishing in.

He chided himself even as he grabbed the life jacket and tugged the door back open. He was surely over-reacting, a hazard of his job that often left him expecting the worst. Maybe a new family had checked in. It was probably kids messing around excitedly as they raced to the water's edge.

As soon as he stepped out of the shack, he realized that wasn't the case. A woman and a girl were hopping into his boat. He'd left it unattended for only a moment because the campground was more or less deserted this early in the season. He regretted that decision now as the woman went straight for the outboard motor and gave the starter rope a powerful tug.

"Hey!" He strode across the grass, waving an arm at them. "That's my boat!" he shouted, just in case she mistakenly thought it was owned by the campground and there for the taking. It could be an honest mistake, because the campground did own a canoe and several kayaks.

The woman gave another powerful yank, ignoring him, even as the young girl stared at him in what looked like fear. He didn't know much about kids, but he'd guess she was around six or seven. She was much too young to be an accomplice to a crime. Both had slight frames and ebony hair. They were probably mother and daughter. He hadn't seen the girl at the campground, but he had noticed the woman a few times since she'd checked in the day before last, though he hadn't paid much attention to her.

In the few seconds it took him to assess the situation, their features were imprinted in his memory, in case he needed to make a statement later.

When it became clear the woman didn't care the boat was his, he took off running. His long legs easily covered the ground between him and the dock, and his feet were soon pounding against the rickety wooden slats as he raced toward his boat.

"Hey, you! Stop!" he shouted again.

The girl unlashed the rope that held the boat to the dock. With another yank, the woman managed to get his cantankerous motor to chug to life. The boat spurted forward.

Jesse made a split-second decision. He launched himself off the dock, knowing if he missed the boat, the worst that could happen was that he'd end up neck-deep in frigid water.

His feet landed with a solid thud in the boat, causing the small vessel to tilt precariously. The edges dipped dangerously close to the water, nearly capsizing before rocking back again. The thieves both reached for the sides of the boat to steady themselves.

"What do you think you're doing?" he demanded. He fought to keep his balance as the deck beneath him continued to rock. "Didn't you hear me? This is my boat."

"Get down!" The woman gave the command, but not to him.

The child ducked, and Jesse was shocked to see two gunmen taking aim at them from the shore.

Where had they come from?

He pushed the woman to the floor, along with her companion. The boat was already pulling away from the shoreline. Bullets pelted into the water around them. He wasn't alerted by the sound of the guns, but by the ripples that resulted from the missed shots landing in the water. The boat's old motor was loud, but not loud enough to drown out gunshots. The men must be using silencers. He needed to get this duo to safety.

He glanced over his shoulder as he crouched down and took over the woman's spot at his motor. He opened the throttle as far as it would go, and the boat zipped toward the center of the lake. He tried to get a good look at the men as he steered. Both were stocky, one a bit taller than the other. Both had sunglasses on and ball caps pulled low. He couldn't see much of their features from this distance. They were dressed in dark jeans and work boots, and one wore what appeared to be a brown leather jacket, while the other had on a dark hoodie.

Shots continued to pelt the water. Some landing dangerously close. With each shot fired, his spine stiffened, and his heart pounded a little harder as he anticipated a direct hit to either the boat or passengers, but every shot fell short. He found it strange the men weren't able to hit the side of a boat. Not exactly a small target, even if it was moving.

What kind of thugs were they?

Yet the fact remained, they had guns and weren't opposed to using them. And for some reason, they were after a woman and child. Jesse wasn't going to stick around and take the chance that one of the wild shots would find its mark. Just then, a bullet pinged against the gunwale of the boat, tearing the trim and leaving a hole along the upper edge. The woman cried out in surprise and wrapped her body around the child.

Jesse veered hard to the left, hoping to throw the gunmen off. It didn't take a lead detective to deduce this pair hadn't stolen his boat to take it for a joyride.

They'd been running for their lives.

"Please," the woman begged, "get us out of here." Huge cornflower blue eyes pleaded silently as she swiped a thick lock of long dark hair out of her face.

"That's the plan," Jesse grumbled. He continued to crouch, making himself as small as possible. "Get the life vest on the kid," he commanded.

He'd dropped it on the floor of the boat as soon as he'd realized there was a problem. If they took another hit, if a bullet punctured the hull and they began taking on water, he wanted to make sure the young girl had at least that protection before they went down. The woman complied, keeping both of their bodies hidden from the men on the shore.

The boat quickly sped them out of range. Jesse maneuvered out of the bay, and within minutes, they were out of the gunmen's view. The water was choppier here, and the small boat bumped and jolted with each wave it crested. Under normal circumstances, he wouldn't take the vessel out of the seclusion of the calm bay.

"You can sit up now," he said. He fought to steer the boat as the harsh waves tried to tear them off course.

The woman cautiously peered over the side of the boat, as if unsure she could trust his judgment. Apparently satisfied they were safe for the moment, she moved to a seated position on the floor, resting her back against the bench seat. The girl scrambled up next to her, and the woman pulled her into her side, sliding a protective arm around her shoulders.

Jesse did a quick scan of the secluded lake. They were the only ones out on the water. Not really a surprise this time of year. A few houses dotted the shoreline, most of them summer homes that would remain abandoned for another month or so. However, he knew if he continued along the eastern side, as he was doing, he'd come upon a public access where he could dock his boat and try to place a call for help. He knew from experience he sure couldn't get any reception out here on the open water.

In the meantime, he needed to figure out what was going on. It was clear that lives depended on it.

Paige Bennett pulled her niece a little closer. The life jacket wrapped around her felt bulky. Paige was grateful that this stranger—a man she'd seen around the campground once or twice but had never spoken to—had thought to have her put it on. It gave her one less thing to worry about. If the boat went down, Molly would be safe. The child trembled in her arms. Paige knew exactly how she felt. Her heart was still pounding out a frantic beat. It was nothing short of miraculous that they had been saved. She breathed a silent prayer of thanks.

While washing the breakfast dishes, she'd noticed a strange car through the window over the kitchen sink. At first, she'd assumed someone was checking in. When the car parked several cabins down, she hadn't given it much thought, until she saw two men climb out of it and head her way. Each had a pistol in his hand, partially hidden but visible all the same. She'd darted across the small living space to where Molly sat reading on the couch.

Molly had noted the fear on her face and leaped up. Together, they'd raced out the back door. Paige hadn't been sure where to go. Her first thought was to dart into the forest, where they could hide. Spotting the boat had caused a spontaneous change of plan.

Now, as she stared up at the man's thunderous expression, she wondered if they'd traded one danger for another.

"What's going on here?" He narrowed his coffee-colored eyes at her. His gaze was intense. Cheekbones that looked as if they were carved from granite made him seem intimidating, though Paige thought he'd have her swooning under other circumstances.

Her mind went into a tailspin. What should she say? What could she say? She felt Molly stiffen in her arms.

"Those men are after us," Paige replied.

He raised an eyebrow and gave her a stern look. "Yeah. I got that much. I need you to elaborate. Who are they?"

"I don't know." That, at least, was the truth. She didn't know who the men were specifically. Though she had a hunch about who had sent them.

"Look, lady," he continued, raking a hand through his dark windblown hair, "those men shot at us after you stole my boat. I think I deserve an explanation."

"I'm sorry about the boat," she said. "I didn't intend to steal it. I would've gotten it back to you somehow." That was the absolute truth.

His scrutinizing gaze swept over her. "At this point, I really don't care about my boat. Men shooting at us," he said pointedly, "that has my attention." He deftly steered the watercraft over the choppy waves, keeping them on course. "We should reach a public access in a few minutes. I'll dock there. Hopefully, I can get some reception and get a deputy out here. You have to start answering some questions."

"Sure. Right." Paige nodded, because what else could she do? She hadn't had much help from law enforcement the past few weeks, but she wasn't going to bother telling him that. In fact, she didn't know what she should tell him.

Should she tell this stranger that her sister, Lydia, had been killed in a car wreck that she was certain wasn't an accident? Or tell him that she suspected her brother-in-law, Molly's stepfather, was behind it?

She could also tell him she was pretty sure someone had broken into her home. No, they hadn't taken anything. Yes, she was aware the local police seemed to think she was being paranoid because nothing was missing, but things had just been out of place. Her whole house had felt *off*, as if it had been carefully rummaged through and not put back together quite right. And what about the beige sedan she was sure had followed her out of town? It was only by the grace of God and a train's providential timing that she'd managed to lose what she was sure was a tail.

Now that she thought about it, that beige car that had followed her had looked an awful lot like the one that had rolled into the campground with the gunmen.

The problem was, she had no proof. Not about any of it. The longer she'd spent in the cabin by the lake, the more she'd started to question herself. She'd started to wonder if perhaps, as the kind police officer had suggested when taking her statement in her kitchen, she was just being paranoid.

Then the gunmen showed up.

She didn't have a clue as to how they had found her. She hadn't used her credit cards. She didn't know if people really were traced that way, but she'd seen it in enough movies to think twice about them. The owners of the campground had been perfectly happy taking cash. Presumably so they wouldn't have to pay the fees credit cards charged. She and Molly had been at the cabin two nights now. So how had Abe Winslow, Lydia's husband, found them?

What had she done wrong?

"Let's back up a bit," he said, cutting into her reverie. "My name's Jesse McGrath. I checked in at the campground several days before you. I've seen you around once or twice. I haven't seen her, though." He nodded his head toward Molly. "How about we start with your names?"

"My name is Paige Bennett. This is my niece, Molly. She hasn't been feeling well, so she's been staying inside. That's why you haven't seen her." Not feeling well? If that wasn't an understatement, Paige didn't know what was. She wasn't going to go into details about the accident Molly was still recovering from. That was none of this man's business. Even if she had attempted to borrow his boat.

"Well, Paige, I'd say it's nice to meet you, but under the circumstances, I'm not so sure about that." Jesse frowned before continuing. "Tell me why those men were coming after you."

Paige clenched her jaw. She didn't want to get into that. Not here. Not now. Not with Molly trembling in fear. Her niece had been through enough. She gazed at him, silently begging him to stop pressing the matter.

He looked at her expectantly.

She cast a sidelong glance at her niece, willing him to understand her hesitation. Molly was already traumatized enough. Though he had no way of knowing how severely her niece was suffering, he seemed to realize that Paige didn't want to discuss the situation in front of her. When she met his gaze again, he gave her a subtle nod and a pointed look. She wasn't off the hook.

"How much farther?" Paige asked.

"It's just up there." He pointed straight ahead. "There's a break in the tree line. You can see the gravel approach leading to the dock. I'll tie my boat up there. There should be strong enough reception to get a call through," he said. "I might have to walk up to the road where the trees are less dense, though. I'll get someone to pick us up. Hopefully, we won't have to wait too long."

She nodded, unsure of what else to say. Though the sun was beaming in the sky, the air was chilled. They had left the cabin so quickly, she hadn't had time to grab jackets. It was frigid out here on the water. That should probably be the least of her concerns, but when Molly shuddered against the cold, her heart nearly broke.

She didn't know what she was going to do next. They'd have to go back to the cabin. Her purse was there. And her car. Would the gunmen wait there for them? Could she take Molly to hide out somewhere else? Would Lydia's husband just find her again? She couldn't imagine what he wanted from her. But she was sure he was behind this.

Paige didn't believe in coincidences. And the fact that

her estranged sister died shortly after sending a copy of her newly created will that made Paige Molly's guardian was too blatant a statement for anyone to ignore.

"It's going to be okay," she murmured to Molly, hoping that it was true. Sending up a quick prayer, begging God to make it so.

Her niece's light blue eyes searched hers. Eyes so much like Lydia's, so much like her own. Paige forced a reassuring smile. Molly didn't say a word.

Not that Paige had expected her to.

"We're just about there," Jesse said. He made a few adjustments, and the boat began to slow. Waves lapped against the sides as he maneuvered them to the shore. With a practiced hand, he eased the boat next to the dock. He cut the engine and grabbed a dock pole. He swiftly wrapped the rope around the pole before hopping out.

Paige and Molly, not nearly as comfortable on the water as Jesse, staggered to their feet. The boat rocked precariously against the waves rushing to the shore. He held out a hand, first steadying Molly as she climbed out of the boat, then Paige.

She glanced around, feeling unnerved by the seclusion. Though it was a public access, it looked as if it was rarely used. There were trees on three sides, and the lake on the fourth. A narrow gravel drive, more like an old trail, snaked up an incline, presumably leading to a main road.

"I'm going to go closer to the road," Jesse said as he studied his phone. "Maybe I'll have better reception at a higher point. I'm going to try to get a call through. If I can't, I'll see if I can get a text out." He paused.

"Worst-case scenario, we might have to hike for a bit. Are you up for it?"

Paige turned to Molly with a questioning look. "We might have to walk for a while. Do you think you can make it?"

With a determined look, Molly nodded.

"I forgot you said she wasn't feeling well," Jesse admitted. "Let's not worry about that yet. Hopefully, I can reach someone. You two stay put. I'll be right back."

With long strides, he hurried up the gravel path that was barely wide enough for a vehicle. Paige maneuvered Molly out of the life jacket and placed it back in the boat.

"He seems like a nice guy," she said, more to assure her niece than for any other reason. He seemed gruff and a little perturbed, but who wouldn't be after having their boat nearly stolen and being shot at by two brutes? "He's going to help us."

Could he help them?

She sure hoped so.

Her heart lurched when she spotted Jesse racing back down the incline.

"Into the woods!" he shouted, pointing as he ran. "Now!"

It was then that Paige heard the hum of a vehicle approaching. It was in the distance but sounded as if it was moving fast.

She grabbed Molly's hand and tugged her along, racing for the tree line with Jesse close behind.

TWO

"How do you know it's the guys who are after us?" Paige asked over her shoulder as she darted ahead of him.

"I don't, not for sure," Jesse admitted as they entered the forest. "Judging by the amount of dust the car's kicking up, they're moving fast. Too fast for normal traffic on this road. There's not much down here other than this access, and they're not pulling any kind of watercraft. They could live in one of the lake houses, but most of them are deserted this early in the season."

"Shouldn't we have just taken your boat?" Paige asked.

"No, it's nearly out of gas." He hadn't wanted to mention it while they were still out on the water, but he hadn't been sure they were going to make it to the access. He'd only planned on fishing in the bay, being anchored in place for the afternoon. He hadn't intended to circle half the lake with the boat going full throttle. He certainly hadn't planned on fighting against the waves and the wind.

They *had* made it to the landing. However, it would

be foolish to try to make another getaway in it at this point.

The crunch of tires on gravel cut through the air, and he knew their pursuers had turned into the boat access.

"We've got to keep moving," he said. "Stay parallel to the shoreline so we don't get lost in these woods."

Paige led the way with Molly right behind her. He stayed behind Molly, ready to assist if she began to lag behind. The sounds of the underbrush crackling and rustling nearly drowned out the sound of the car winding down the gravel path.

Though they'd gotten a good head start, he cringed when he heard car doors slam. He hoped their pursuers would waste valuable seconds trying to decide which way to go.

"There's the boat!" one of the men shouted. "I'll go that way!"

He didn't hear the other man's much more subdued reply. Again, he wondered what kind of thugs these were. Stealth was clearly not their specialty.

He wished he knew which direction they were headed, because despite the shout, he wasn't sure. Were the men guessing or had they managed to track them that quickly? Had they seen trampled underbrush? Broken branches?

He didn't know.

"If we keep moving," he said, his voice low as they raced along, "we'll eventually stumble onto someone's property." He visualized the last dock they'd seen. His best guess was that the house was half a mile away. Not all that far on a normal trek, but through the woods, it would take them a while.

"I'm not sure we can make it that far," Paige said as

she glanced over her shoulder to check on Molly. The young girl staggered, and Jesse reached out to catch her. He looped his hand around her waist and pulled her back to her feet before her knees collided with the forest floor.

"She was in a car accident not too long ago," Paige explained. "She's not in any condition to run."

That was all the information Jesse needed. He scooped Molly up, holding her in the crook of his arm as he took off again. The girl was light, and running with her wasn't a burden. He looked back but didn't catch sight of their pursuers. Were they right behind them? In danger of catching up? He had no idea if they were even headed this way.

Paige was already beginning to slow. Molly was so dainty that he barely noticed her weight, not with the adrenaline coursing through his veins. Even so, he worried that the two unencumbered men would catch up sooner rather than later.

Or at least one of them. It made sense for the two men to split up, meaning that at least one of them had to be on their tail.

He made a split-second decision and hoped it was the right one.

"Paige," he said under his breath.

She slowed as she glanced back at him.

"We need to hide." He held Molly steady with one hand and grabbed Paige by the elbow with the other. He ushered them toward the water. A huge, ancient balsam had fallen, landing in the lake. It wasn't ideal, but it was the best he could come up with.

"We're going in. The tree will provide coverage." Her brow furrowed, but he didn't wait for her to argue. He had Molly, and he knew Paige would follow where she went. He rushed to the lake's edge and into the water.

The water was icy, still chilled from the winter. Molly's body went rigid, and a whimper crept out of her mouth.

"I know, kiddo," he tried to soothe. "But just trust me on this."

Trust him?

That was asking a lot, he knew.

Please, let this be the right decision. Please, help me keep these two safe.

He was startled by his plea. Who was he speaking to? Surely not God. He and God had never really been on speaking terms. He shoved the thought aside. No time to ponder it now. Not when their lives were on the line.

They waded through weeds and lily pads, their feet sticking in the muck, making it hard to move into deeper water quickly. But Paige didn't complain. Molly didn't make a peep. He expected her to protest, say the water was too cold, or something. But she remained mute as they waded deeper, and the water crept ever higher. It was so cold, it nearly took his breath away. He hated dragging these two into its depths, but he saw no other way.

He reached the middle of the fallen tree. The dead reddish needles were thick among the branches. The water was well past his waist and up to Paige's chest. She reached for Molly, and the girl leaned away from him and slid into Paige's arms. Paige held her easily, her weight buoyed by the water, keeping her head clear of the waves rolling in.

Instinctively, they all moved into the tree, seeking refuge in the thick branches covered in dead orange needles. The boughs were so thick they nearly obscured his view of the shore.

That was good. It meant their pursuer's view of them would be obscured as well. Hopefully, he wouldn't think to look in the water and wouldn't even glance their way.

Paige turned to him, a question in her expression.

He pressed a finger to his lips and nodded in the direction they'd come.

"Did you find them?" The gruff voice carried through the woods, nearly shouting. They were likely struggling with poor reception. "Me neither," he grumbled after a moment, his voice growing louder as he neared. "Maybe they cut back and crossed the road." There was a stretch of silence, and then he said, "I don't know what to do! You tell me! You were so keen on making decisions back at the campground. I told you we should go in on foot. Sneak up on the cabin. But no, you didn't listen. You had to drive in there like you owned the place. Gave her the chance to spot us."

Jesse craned his neck, trying to see through the branches. He saw the man's profile as he held a phone to his ear. He couldn't make out any distinguishing features. The man's hair was still hidden by his baseball cap. Dark sunglasses covered a portion of his face. His brown leather jacket stretched across broad shoulders. Something glittered. An earring? Jesse thought so. He also thought he could make out a tattoo creeping up the guy's neck, though he couldn't make out what it was.

"We could run through these woods all day and never find them," he argued. He paused a moment and then said, "I am looking. You want me to do what? Wait. I can't hear you." He held out his phone, as if looking to see how much reception he had. He took a few steps, then put the phone back to his ear. "What now?"

Jesse felt Paige and Molly stiffen. But they were so quiet, he couldn't even hear them breathing over the sound of the waves sloshing against the shoreline.

As the goon headed their way, Jesse fought the urge to try to get a better look at his face. He knew he shouldn't. Any movement would be unwise. Instead, he had to settle for the limited view through the foliage.

"How am I supposed to know where they went?" he growled. "I'm only doing what you told me to do! You know I don't like this. I didn't want any part of it. I know we aren't supposed to hurt the kid, but you're a horrible shot and you could've hit her accidentally. I don't want no part of that. Do you hear me? Going after a lady is bad enough. I don't care how much money you were promised. Prison time isn't worth it. Besides, I don't want no blood on my conscience. I'm leaving that up to you!"

He heard Paige's slight intake of breath, but fortunately, Molly remained silent. Her eyes widened with fear. Her expression yanked at Jesse's heart. He wanted to reassure her somehow but couldn't risk it.

The thug was quiet as he paced back and forth, presumably getting an earful from the man on the other end. "I know you blame me for the deal that went bad in Denver. You don't let me forget. But let me tell you something. I never wanted to do this kinda gig." He pivoted again.

Adrenaline spiked through Jesse as he instinctively reached for the weapon he didn't have. In that moment, he was sure the gunman's gaze linked with his through the layers of balsam boughs. But the moment came and went in the blink of an eye. Then the man walked away, grumbling into his phone once more.

"I'm telling ya, they had too much of a head start. And we don't even know which direction they went. They might've even crossed the road and run into the field. I say we call this a bust." He tromped off into the woods, his voice fading the farther he went, drowned out by the sound of branches cracking and breaking under his feet.

Paige slowly released the breath she'd been holding. Molly turned to her. The child's expression was etched with fear.

"It'll be okay," Paige whispered.

The water was cold. So, so cold. She knew Molly had to be freezing. She wasn't sure how much longer they could take it. Her niece's teeth began to chatter, and her body shuddered. Paige was utterly miserable and knew Molly and Jesse must be, too.

But they were alive. Thank God, they were still alive.

"We need to get out of here," Jesse said, keeping his tone low as well. "I don't dare go back the way we came, just in case one of them stays behind. It's already chilly out, and now that we're wet, we need to get dry as soon as possible. Moving at a steady clip will help us to warm up."

Paige didn't argue. She could tell Molly was about at her limit for the day. The girl should be resting, not running through the woods, afraid for her life. Not hiding in frigid water to escape men with guns.

At least the brute didn't want Molly hurt. It was a small blessing, but it was something.

Jesse disentangled them from the balsam boughs

they'd been hiding in. Pointing down the shoreline, he said, "That house isn't too far away."

They hadn't been able to see the house while running through the woods. But from this vantage point in the water, she realized he was right. Once on dry land again, they could make it there in a matter of minutes.

"What if the men head that way?" Paige asked.

"We'll watch for their car," Jesse said. "I don't plan on actually going up to the house. You'll stay in the woods while I check the mailbox number so I can figure out our exact location. We don't have a lot of options here," he reminded her. "It's cold, and we need to get into dry clothes."

"I'm so sorry we dragged you into this," Paige said.

"Don't be," he replied as he motioned for them to move toward the shore. "It seems the two of you need someone on your side."

An engine started in the distance. She hoped that meant both men were taking off. A moment later, the car drove away. Whether the car left as a ruse, leaving one of the men behind, or whether they had given up, she didn't know.

"But what if they figure out who you are?" Paige asked as they waded to the shore. "I'm sure they noticed your boat tied to the dock. They probably took the registration off it."

"Let them try to figure it out." Jesse smirked. "Maybe once they know who I am, they'll back off."

His words held Paige in place. She paused several feet from the shoreline, muck up to her ankles, water streaming down her body. Molly stopped next to her, her small body trembling. "What do you mean? Who are you?"

"I've been on vacation this past week, but I'm a deputy with the Cascade Falls Sheriff's Department."

Paige clenched her jaw to keep from saying something snarky. He was a deputy? She wasn't sure how she felt about that. She knew she should be relieved, but given her recent experience with law enforcement, she probably shouldn't expect him to be a whole lot of help.

Despite what he'd just done.

"You sure didn't go far from home to take a vacation," Paige said. The Hideaway was a rustic resort out in a rural area, and she'd needed to use a map for directions. She recalled the campground had a Cascade Falls address, since that was the closest town.

His eyebrow hitched. "I worked here when I was in high school. I happen to like the place, even though it's under new ownership. Besides, I have my reasons for wanting to stick close to my hometown."

He must've realized she was going to ask him about those reasons, because he cut her off.

"Hopefully, they'll come to their senses and decide not to tangle with law enforcement." His tone held assurance, as if he thought that might be a real possibility. She wasn't so sure.

With one hand on Molly's shoulder, she guided her niece out of the water. She hated that Molly was going through this. The child should be home. Warm. Cozy. Safe. She should be with her mother. A wave of emotion washed over Paige as she thought of Lydia. Gone. Leaving Molly motherless.

Her niece was already fatherless, her dad having died when she was an infant.

Molly was her responsibility now.

And so far, she hadn't exactly done what she considered a stellar job. Just look at them. Hiding out at a campground. Shot at. Soaking wet. And with danger looming that she didn't understand.

She glanced at Jesse. He was studying her with a fierce look on his face. Perhaps she could count on him for some help. It was his job, after all.

Once they were all on dry land, they began their trek toward the house Jesse had pointed out. Molly was walking this time but shivering, and Paige was worried about how this would affect her recovery. Then again, if the men had found them, recovery would be the least of her concerns. She was fairly certain if the men had caught up to them, she'd be dead. And Molly? She shuddered. The gunman had said they didn't want the girl hurt. But what would they do with her? Would they do anything? Or was it just Paige they were after, and Molly was an innocent bystander? Would they return her to Abe, her stepfather? Was that what this was about? Did he want her back? Did he think he needed to get Paige out of the picture so that Molly would have nowhere else to go? Oh, how she wished she knew.

She couldn't think of that right now. She needed to concentrate on the present. Jesse was right. They needed dry clothes. They needed to warm up. They needed rest. A hot meal sure wouldn't hurt.

Molly's body shuddered as a bout of shivering overtook her. She pushed ahead, trudging through the forest, putting one foot in front of the other. Carrying on just as she had in the weeks since her mother's death. Paige's only sibling had been killed in a horrific car accident. The very same accident that, by the grace of God, Molly had survived.

This poor child had been through so much already.

She should be allowed to mourn for her mother in peace. Instead, they were on the run from the man Paige was sure had taken Lydia's life.

"We're almost there, I think," Jesse said. Paige glanced back. He had his phone raised in the air. "Help is on the way," he announced.

"How do you know?" Paige demanded. She hadn't heard him call anyone.

"I didn't have time to try to get a call to go through, but I sent a text when I saw those guys crest the hill in their car. Erin—that's my sister—responded. Her text said she left right away She's not as familiar with the area as I am, and I doubt she knows where the access is. I'll send her an update on our exact location once I get a look at the mailbox number." He paused—apparently doing some mental mathematics—then said, "She should be here within the next ten minutes."

Molly stopped, turned to Paige and pointed in the direction they'd been headed. The house they'd seen from their hiding spot in the lake was now visible through the trees.

"Yes." Paige nodded her encouragement. "We're almost there."

"Let's skirt the property," Jesse said. "If those men are lurking, I don't want to be out in the open."

In minutes, they reached the road. Jesse ordered them to stay out of sight within the tree line while he got a look at the mailbox number. Paige kept track of him as he crept along the edge of the trees, watching for traffic. It was a quiet country road, and no one seemed to be around. He darted to the mailbox.

Paige slid her arm around Molly's waist. The child

leaned into her, resting her weight against Paige, her head on her chest. She released a weary sigh.

"Hang in there, sweetie. We'll be out of here soon," Paige told her. She pressed a kiss on the top of Molly's head.

She received no response, but she hadn't expected one. Other than one short sentence, Molly hadn't spoken since the accident.

She watched as Jesse tapped out a text on his phone. He hurried back, joining them where they stood out of sight.

"She's close," he informed them. "I told her that if another car's in sight, she should keep going and loop back around when she's able. I don't want to take any chances."

Paige met his gaze, forcing as much feeling into her words as she could muster. "Thank you."

She wanted to say thank you for getting them across the lake. Thank you for finding them somewhere to hide. Thank you for arranging for someone to rescue them.

She said none of those things out loud. She was afraid she wouldn't be able to keep the tremor from her voice. She didn't want her niece any more rattled than she was. While they were out of danger for now, she feared it wouldn't last. The men had found her before. She didn't doubt they'd be able to find her again.

The sound of gravel crunching under tires alerted her to a vehicle coming their way.

Jesse's phone pinged with an incoming text.

"That's Erin," he said. "Stay back until I'm sure the coast is clear."

Paige and Molly followed his order as a silver SUV

rumbled down the road, slowing as it neared the driveway. Jesse stepped out of the woods, and the vehicle skidded to a stop.

The window rolled down, and a woman who looked nothing like Jesse narrowed her green eyes at them. Her curly blond hair swung in her ponytail when she said, "What kind of trouble did you get yourself into now?"

"No time to chat," Jesse replied. Paige didn't miss how his gaze constantly scoured the road in both directions, watching for their attackers. He ushered Paige and Molly up the small embankment. He opened the back door and allowed them to scramble in. Then he jogged around to the passenger side.

Erin corkscrewed her neck, getting a good look at Paige and Molly in the back seat. Her friendly smile slipped into a look of concern. "You're sopping wet. You've got to be freezing. Let me turn up the heat."

"I'll turn up the heat," Jesse said. "You just drive."

Paige buckled up and made sure Molly did, too. The warm blast of air was almost immediate, and she was grateful.

Jesse made quick introductions, not giving any more information than their names.

"Take us back to the Hideaway Campground," he requested.

"Are you sure that's a good idea?" Paige demanded as she leaned forward, putting her head between the front seats. "What if they went back there?"

He flashed her a grin that held no humor. "I don't think that's likely. But I sure hope they did. I sent out a few texts to my fellow deputies. They'll meet us there. At the very least, they're going to need to take our statements. I want to look around, see if they left any evidence behind. The more info we can give the authorities, the better chance we'll have at catching those guys."

He had a point. Besides, they all needed to change into dry clothes, so it made sense to go back to the cabins. She leaned back in her seat and slid an arm around Molly, pulling her close. Glancing over her shoulder, she saw the road behind them was still empty. They were safe for now.

But how long would it last?

THREE

Paige hadn't thought going back to the campground was the best idea. Not that she had a better one. But when she saw a cruiser and realized two deputies had already arrived, she felt some of her tension ease.

She wasn't surprised when Jesse directed Erin to the cabin she and Molly were staying in. There were only a few other guests at the campground. She'd recognized him from cabin 4.

"I see Deputy Chad Harris down by the beach, blocking it off as a crime scene," Jesse told her. "And that's the sheriff, Gloria Sanchez, speaking with the campground owners." He glanced over his shoulder. "She's going to want to question us next."

"How long do you think her questioning will take?" Paige asked. "I'd like to pack up and get on the road as soon as possible."

"It could take a while," Jesse said evasively. "Where are you planning on going?"

That was a good question. She had nearly depleted her cash supply. She'd have to hit up an ATM. And then what? She could only hide out for so long.

"I don't know," she said. Her gaze drifted down to

Molly. "I'll figure something out. Everything will be just fine."

She didn't miss the concerned glance Erin shot Jesse.

"You two go change into dry clothes," Jesse said as he opened his door. "I'm going to check in quick with the sheriff and then I'll do the same. We'll come back to your cabin to get your statement." He hopped out and strode toward his boss.

Erin said, "I'm just going to stick around for a while."

"Thanks for all of your help," Paige replied.

"Of course." She gave Paige a sympathetic smile.

"Come on, sweetheart." Paige took Molly by the hand. The child was shivering, and Paige felt like a complete failure as a guardian. So far, she had provided her niece no stability at all. Molly obediently slid out of the vehicle. She hadn't taken the time to lock the door, so she was able to usher Molly right into the cabin.

With a glance over her shoulder, she noted that Jesse had finished talking to Sheriff Sanchez and was headed to his own cabin two down from hers.

Once inside, she led Molly into the bedroom that held two double beds.

She knelt down in front of her, looking the child in the eyes. "How are you doing?"

Molly shrugged.

Paige pulled her in for a hug. She held her niece close and stroked her hair. "I love you, sweetie. I know everything seems a little crazy right now. But I promise I'm going to take care of you."

Please, God, she begged with her whole heart. *Please help me to take care of her. Please help me to keep her safe.*

"Can you get yourself into dry clothes?" Paige asked.

Molly nodded and took the outfit Paige handed her.

"I'm going to go change in the bathroom," Paige told her. "Then I'm going to turn the gas fireplace on. You can curl up with a movie for a little while, okay? That'll help you warm up."

Molly didn't reply.

With a sigh, she grabbed a change of clothes for herself and headed to the bathroom. She'd love a warm shower, and Molly would need one, too. But she had a feeling her statement couldn't wait. She was just tugging a dry sweater over her head when she heard a knock on the door. She hustled across the cabin feeling completely unprepared to answer questions of any kind. The past few weeks had been a roller coaster of emotions, and she didn't think she was going to be hitting an even keel anytime soon.

She was surprised to find Erin standing at the door. The woman gave her a sheepish smile.

"Hey there," Erin said. "I know you have to speak with the sheriff. I thought maybe I could stay with Molly. You could meet over in Jesse's cabin for some privacy."

Paige heard Molly shuffle out of the bedroom. She hesitated, not terribly comfortable leaving Molly with a stranger. But she was even less comfortable thinking that Molly might overhear what she had to say.

"Chad said he'd stay here with Molly and me," Erin said. "He'll make sure we're safe. Gloria will question you and Jesse. I know both Chad and Gloria. They're good people. They'll do what they can to help find who did this. What do you think? Are you okay leaving Molly with me?"

Paige turned to Molly. "I need to go speak with one of the deputies we saw outside. They have a few questions for me. I promise to be back as soon as I can. Erin said she'll stay with you here. Is that okay?"

Molly hesitated, nodded slowly, and then her eyes drifted to the television.

"I told her she could watch a movie," Paige told Erin. "We packed a few in her bag. Molly—" she returned her attention to her niece "—would you please go pick what you want to watch?"

Molly nodded again and shuffled away.

"Thank you again," Paige said. "Hopefully, I won't be gone too long."

Erin reached out and squeezed her hand. "Take as long as you need. Chad's right outside the door. Molly will be just fine."

Paige blew out a breath. "Okay. I better go get this over with."

Then she needed to make a plan. Because they surely couldn't stay here another night. She couldn't return home either. So where was she going to go?

"Please stop looking at me like that," Jesse grumbled to the sheriff.

She dropped down into a chair across the table from him. She already had a notebook out and a pen ready. They were just waiting for Paige.

"How am I looking at you?" Sheriff Sanchez asked, her brown eyes sparkling. She wasn't even trying to hide her smirk. "A week ago, you tried to give me your resignation. You told me you don't think law enforcement is right for you anymore. Yet here you are, on vacation, rescuing a lady and kid, whisking them off to safety, helping them escape not one, but two active shooters. Did I mention you did this while on vacation?"

He scrubbed a hand over his face. Now was not the time to think about his ex. Trish had conned him, and if things had gone differently, she could've cost him his job. As it was, thanks to her, he couldn't help second-guessing himself now. He shoved thoughts of her, and the theft ring she had been a part of, aside.

"Law enforcement is in your blood," she said, her tone going serious. "You're good at what you do, and we need you. Don't walk away from a career you love because of one bad experience."

He didn't want to talk about that particular experience, the disastrous relationship with Trish that had caused him to take his first vacation in three years. The sheriff had told him she had no interest in letting him quit. She'd told him to take some time to clear his head instead. So much for that.

"You figured out what Trish was up to," she continued, squelching his hope that she was going to let this drop.

"But I dated her for *months*," he grumbled. Trish was constantly asking about his job, questioning the cases he was working on. He'd thought she was genuinely interested and had no idea she was pumping him for useful details. "She was trying to get information from me, and I didn't even realize it. I was a fool."

Not to mention he felt like a failure as a deputy. He should have realized what she was up to. Part of his job was reading people, and he'd failed miserably.

Gloria's gaze turned serious. "No one thinks you're a fool. You figured her out in the end. And we took down the theft ring because of it."

He was relieved when Paige knocked on the cabin's door.

"Come on in!" he called.

She opened the door and took a hesitant step inside. Jesse made quick introductions, and Paige seemed to relax a bit at the sheriff's kind smile and calm demeanor.

"Did Erin stay with Molly?" he asked. He knew Erin was going to suggest it. He had hoped that Paige would agree in case the questioning became intense.

"She did. It was nice of her to offer," Paige said as she took a seat at the table.

"So, Paige," Gloria began, "Jesse briefed me, but I'd like to hear your full version of events."

Paige nodded.

"First off, any idea who the men were?" Gloria asked.

Paige bit her bottom lip.

Why was she hesitating? Was she hiding something? Or was he simply being suspicious, overly cautious because of the ordeal Trish had just put him through? He wasn't sure, but he wasn't about to let another pretty lady take advantage of him. Trish had been a liar, and he'd been a fool to buy into her tale. He had no desire to go through that again. No. He wouldn't fall for the damsel-in-distress charade. Although, he had to admit, he knew this was no charade. The flying bullets attested to that.

Finally, she shook her head. "Not really."

"Not really?" Jesse asked. He'd been impatiently waiting to hear her account of events, only biding his time because he hadn't wanted to question her in front of Molly. But they'd been shot at. They'd been chased through the woods. Someone clearly wanted Paige dead, and all she had was *not really*?

He realized that Sheriff Sanchez was giving him a look. Right. He was on vacation. She was in charge here.

She cleared her throat and returned her attention to Paige. "You don't sound so sure about that."

Paige wrapped her arms tightly around herself, as if still trying to warm up. Or perhaps she was just trying to hold herself together. An unbidden urge to pull her into a hug hit him hard. But only because she was chilled and scared. It wasn't anything more than that, for sure, he told himself. It wasn't because, in that moment, she looked delicate and fragile, and his chivalrous urge to protect was kicking in.

"I don't know who they are exactly," she admitted. "But I think I know who sent them."

"Who?" Jesse demanded. He winced, feeling his supervisor's gaze slice into him without having to look her way. He leaned back in his seat and tried to keep his mouth shut.

"Who?" Gloria asked.

"I think it would be best if I backed up a little bit," Paige answered. "My sister—her name was Lydia Winslow—was killed in a car accident earlier this month. She appointed me as Molly's guardian should anything happen to her."

"Where did the accident take place?" Gloria asked, her tone gentle.

"On a rural road just east of Briarville," Paige said, naming a town right outside of Grand Junction, about an hour east of their current location in Cascade Falls. "I live in Grand Junction, so it didn't take me long to get to Molly."

Jesse could tell it took a lot of effort for Paige to speak about her sister's recent death.

Struggling to remain composed, she told them her sister was killed when her car went over an embankment. Molly was in the car, too, strapped tightly into her booster chair in the middle of the back seat. Molly survived with minor injuries, but Lydia did not.

"I'm sure she was leaving her husband that night," Paige admitted. "And I think he killed her for it. And now I think he's after me."

The accusation seemed to echo in the silence that filled the room.

When it became obvious she wasn't going to elaborate, Gloria asked, "You think your sister was murdered?"

Jesse said nothing, though his mind was spinning. It was a pretty big accusation. Yet having someone shoot at you and chase you down was a big deal, too, so he didn't exactly doubt her. But he needed more facts.

Paige nodded. "Molly only sustained minor injuries, but they kept her in the hospital overnight for observation. It was late when I got the call, but I went directly to her. She was sleeping when I arrived. I stayed in her room with her because I didn't want her to be alone when she woke up." She paused, her expression going serious. "When she did wake up, she said, 'Mama said he's trying to kill us.' I asked her who she meant." She paused. Pulled in a breath. Blew it out. "But Abe, her stepfather, came in the room. Her face went pale when she saw him. I can't forget the way she shrank back into her pillow as if she was terrified. Molly hasn't spoken a word since then. The doctor told me it's called traumatic mutism. It's one way her brain is protecting her from an overwhelming situation. I'm hopeful that she'll regain her speech soon, but so far, that hasn't happened."

Realization speared through Jesse. He hadn't thought much about it, thought maybe Molly was just quiet because she was scared or shy around strangers. But now that Paige had pointed it out, he realized that the child had not uttered a single word. Not a single one.

"That's not all," Paige continued. "A few weeks before she died, Lydia created a will. I don't know about you," she said firmly, "but I don't believe in coincidences. I think she knew her life was in danger." She paused as if gathering strength. "I think she thought her husband wanted her dead. And she was right."

"Did you bring this to the attention of the local police?" Jesse asked.

"I did." She frowned, as if it were an unpleasant memory. She told them that she'd brought her suspicions to the Briarville PD, and that they claimed they'd conducted a thorough investigation of the accident and hadn't found any signs of foul play. The damage to the car was consistent with an accident. There were no unexplained dents or paint chips that would indicate Lydia had been hit. The skid marks were indicative of going around the corner too fast and slamming on the brakes too late, causing the car to slide out of control. The front end had slammed into a tree as the car careened down the hill.

Interesting, Jesse thought. It sounded as if the department had done a good job. So perhaps there was more to this story. Was Paige hiding something?

"So, Abe…" Gloria glanced at her notes. "What's his last name?"

"Winslow. Abe Winslow. He's Molly's stepfather."

Gloria looked up from the notes she was taking. "Is Molly's father in the picture?"

"My sister's first husband died when Molly was just three months old," Paige said. "He worked the night shift and was hit by a drunk driver on his way to the factory. Molly's six now."

Gloria made a few notes. "Back to Abe. There were no charges brought against him?"

"None." Paige tapped her hand against the table. "I should also mention he's friends with the mayor of Briarville. He's also a big police supporter. He owns an established construction company, so he's…" She frowned. "He's really wealthy. One of the officers that I spoke with mentioned he donated a substantial amount of protective gear to the department last year."

Gloria studied her for a moment. "Are you saying the department is covering for him?"

Paige quickly shook her head. "I'm not saying that. I'm saying I don't know what to think. But I don't believe my sister's accident was really an accident."

Jesse wondered if maybe she was in denial, still trying to process the tragedy. He'd seen it before. Someone unable to accept that a loved one—especially someone so young—had died senselessly.

"Why did you decide to come here, of all campgrounds?" Jesse asked. "I would think you'd want to get far away from Briarville."

"I want to meet with Rodney Zielinski, Lydia's lawyer. His office is in Cascade Falls," she said.

Jesse nodded, because even though he'd never had dealings with him, he'd heard of the man. He found it interesting that Lydia had chosen a lawyer from out of town. Why would she do that? Was she afraid that if she met with someone closer, someone in Briarville or Grand Junction, that her husband might find out? It was conjecture, of course, but it was a possibility.

"This campground seemed like as good a choice

as any." She winced. "But you're right. I probably should've gone somewhere farther away."

This campground was barely an hour to the west of Briarville, but if she wanted to meet with the lawyer, she had a good reason for choosing this location.

"I'll touch base with the Briarville PD," Gloria stated. "I'll let them know what happened here today."

"Maybe they've come up with something new," Paige replied, though she didn't sound too hopeful.

"I'd like to talk a bit more about possible motive," Gloria said. "Was there strain in your sister's marriage? Abuse?"

Jesse didn't miss how Paige glanced away, almost nervously, before turning her attention back to Gloria. "I hate to say I don't know. My sister and I drifted apart the past few years. That's why it was so surprising to get her note with a copy of the will in the mail."

"What did the note say?" He couldn't help but ask.

"Just that she would be in touch soon." Tears welled in Paige's eyes. "I was looking forward to hearing from her. But a few days later, she was gone."

Despite his hesitancy in trusting Paige, his heart clenched. He didn't think she was faking her heartache. It was almost painful to see.

"There's no motive that you can think of?" Gloria asked, her tone soft.

Paige leaned forward, her voice firm when she said, "This is what I know." She held up her hand and counted the facts off on three fingers. "My sister recently created her will, granting me custody of Molly in the event of her death. Molly told me Lydia said 'he's trying to kill us' only moments before her car went off an embankment. My sister is dead." She dropped her hand to the table. "And now someone is after me. I was *shot* at. Something is clearly going on."

"But Mr. Winslow wasn't one of the men on the beach?" Gloria clarified.

"No. But I mentioned he's quite wealthy," Paige reminded her.

"You think he hired someone?" Gloria asked.

"People were shooting at me," Paige said firmly. "I'm a librarian at a small private high school in Grand Junction. I live alone in a quiet neighborhood." She held up her hands helplessly. "I lived a quiet life up until my sister died. So yes, I believe my sister's death and what happened today are tied together somehow."

Jesse was sure she was right. He just wasn't convinced Abe Winslow was behind it all. The evidence she'd presented was only circumstantial. He needed hard evidence, proof.

"The men on the beach were amateurs," he inserted. "But I think Paige is right about the men being hired."

"Why is that?" Gloria asked.

Jesse leaned forward. "We heard the guy on the phone in the woods. He mentioned a substantial amount of money was involved, implying they were being paid. He said this wasn't his normal type of gig. He also accused the other guy of being a bad shot. Between the two of them, could barely hit the broadside of a boat. Overall, they were sloppy. Showing up here in the middle of the day, shooting in public. The good thing about amateurs is that eventually they leave evidence behind. I'm hoping we catch these guys sooner rather than later."

"I just don't understand how they found me," Paige lamented. "I was so careful. I only used cash."

"Did you use your phone?" Jesse asked.

She frowned, and a small furrow formed between her brows. "I did. This morning. I called Lydia's lawyer. I wanted to talk to him about the will. I didn't expect him to answer on a Sunday morning. I was hoping his voice mail would list office hours because they weren't on his website. I was going to leave a message, requesting a meeting as soon as possible."

"He answered?" Jesse asked.

"He did. He agreed to meet with me tomorrow morning," Paige said.

"That could be how they tracked you," Gloria said. "But someone would have had to have access to your phone at some point to use GPS tracking."

"I suppose that could have happened at the funeral." Her furrow deepened. "I set my purse down in the pew instead of lugging it around with me. I thought it would be safe in a church."

Jesse shared a look with Gloria. Abe Winslow was definitely worth looking into.

"If that's how they found me," Paige said, "my phone won't be an issue anymore. It didn't survive our dunk in the lake."

"We'll look into getting you a new one," Jesse assured her, grateful his own phone was waterproof. Under the circumstances, she shouldn't be without one.

She gave him a grateful nod.

Gloria wrapped up the questioning, then stood. "I'm going to see if Chad got everything he needed down by the beach. Let me know if you remember anything else," she said to both of them.

Then Jesse found himself sitting alone with Paige.

She stood. "I need to get back to Molly."

"I'll walk you."

She didn't argue.

They crossed the short distance to her cabin. Erin had obviously been watching for them, because she came outside and met them on the porch. Chad and Gloria were a few feet away, clearly discussing the case.

"Molly's sleeping. She conked right out," Erin said.

"I'm glad. She's got to be exhausted," Paige murmured.

Erin cocked her head to the side and had a determined look on her face. Jesse instantly wondered what she was up to.

"You should stay with me," Erin offered, her gaze locked on Paige. "You and Molly."

"What?" Paige asked. She shook her head. "We couldn't."

"Yes," Erin said. "You sure can. I have a huge house all to myself. You already said you couldn't stay here and weren't sure where you were going to go. You'll be safe with me. I own a pretty good-sized ranch. It's the perfect place for you to hide out. No one would ever think to look for you there."

Jesse pinched the bridge of his nose a moment while he thought that over. Was there any way for the men to trace them to the ranch? He was sure there had been no traffic on the road when Erin picked them up. And now? All of the vehicles at the campground were accounted for. If the men had been in the vicinity when the sheriff arrived, it was unlikely they'd been foolish enough to stick around.

Still, if they were going to do this, he'd have Erin take a roundabout route home. And he'd be extra vigilant to be sure they weren't followed.

To his surprise, he heard himself say, "She's right. You said you've been using cash. But if you're like me, you don't have endless resources. Besides, this way you'll be nearby if the department has more questions for you."

Erin gave him a raised-eyebrow look. Clearly, she'd been expecting him to protest. Maybe he should, but he didn't like the idea of a woman and child out on their own. Not under these circumstances.

Chad strode over, evidently having heard Erin's offer. "I can take your truck," he said to Jesse. "I'll go get your boat, get it back to your house. We can get the truck back to you by tonight, bring it to the ranch. That way, you all can head out right away."

"I appreciate that," Jesse said. If Paige was going with Erin, he was going along to keep them all safe. Not just for Paige and Molly's sake. If Erin was involved, he was absolutely going to stick around to provide some protection. "When you drop the boat off at my place, would you mind grabbing a few things for me before dropping my truck off?"

"I can do that," Chad agreed. "What do you need?"

Jesse explained to Chad where he kept his weapon and his laptop, thinking both might be wise to have on hand.

Less than half an hour later, both cabins were cleared out. Sheriff Sanchez checked the resort over one final time while Chad left in Jesse's truck. Erin led the way in her SUV. Jesse, Paige and Molly followed Erin in Paige's car.

"It was really gracious of Erin to offer to let us stay with her," Paige said.

"She's just that kind of person," Jesse replied. Erin

had a heart of gold. Of course she'd want to help Paige and Molly. He shouldn't have been surprised by her offer. Later, when he had a chance to speak with her alone, he'd thank her.

Gravel crunched under the tires of Paige's car as the trees started whizzing by. He hated to be a nag about her driving skills, but he was a law enforcement officer. Even off duty, he felt obligated to remind her that safety mattered.

"You might want to slow down," he warned. "This road has lots of curves." Even as the words were leaving his mouth, he realized something.

Paige's foot was pumping the brake pedal. Pumping hard.

They were not slowing down.

"I'm trying," she said, her voice quiet, controlled. Full of fear. Instinctively, he knew she didn't want to frighten Molly, who was buckled into the back seat. "I don't think my brakes are working."

She pumped hard one more time. Under normal circumstances, the car would've ground to a jolting halt. Now it did nothing.

Absolutely nothing.

As they neared a curve in the road, realization slammed into Jesse. Sometime during the day, the men must have cut the brake lines on Paige's car.

The first curve was drawing near.

Paige continued to pump the brakes with no effect.

A small whimper escaped Paige's throat, making Jesse's heart pound.

"What do I do?" she ground out under her breath. Her knuckles were white as she clenched the steering wheel in a death grip. "How do we stop?"

That was an excellent question.

If he didn't figure out a way to slow the vehicle down, they weren't going to survive.

FOUR

Paige steered the car into the curve, tires skidding, gravel flying. She tried stomping on the emergency brake, but it was useless. The entire time, she talked to herself.

No, Jesse realized as he frantically tapped his phone, bringing up Erin's number. She wasn't talking to herself. She was praying.

The phone rang in his ear.

Pick up. Pick up, he willed Erin. She had Bluetooth and could take a hands-free call. On the third ring, her voice came across the line.

"Hello?"

"We have a problem." Wasting no time, he explained what had happened.

"What can I do?" Erin asked, her tone matter-of-fact. Calm and cool as always. He knew that was why she was such a good veterinarian.

He explained what he needed from her and then disconnected so both of his hands were free.

"Did you hear that?" Jesse asked Paige. "Do you understand what you need to do?"

"Yes." Paige's knuckles were still white as they gripped the steering wheel, but she looked determined.

"We won't be on this straight stretch much longer," Jesse warned as Erin's brake lights flashed in front of them. "We have to do this now."

Paige said nothing, just concentrated on Erin's vehicle in front of her.

Jesse twisted in his seat, turning to Molly. "How're you doing, sweetheart?"

Molly's lower lip trembled, but that was the only sign of her fear.

"Hang on tight," he told her. She obediently grabbed the crossbar of her booster seat. He placed one hand against her chest to help secure her, and one on the dash in front of him. He pressed his feet against the floorboards, bracing himself.

The front of Paige's small car made impact with Erin's back bumper, just as he'd instructed. Erin's vehicle seemed to handle the impact well. But the jolt to Paige's car was jarring, tossing them against their seat belts. Paige's car slowed some, though it didn't come to a complete stop. Both vehicles continued their forward trajectories. Erin tapped her brakes again, allowing Paige's car to hit her once more. The impact of the car hitting a moving vehicle headed in the same direction was a lot less dangerous than crashing into something stationary like a tree. Or worse, another car coming at them head-on.

With each tap into the back bumper of Erin's large SUV, Paige's car slowed a little more. Finally, Erin braked slowly with Paige's car pressed up against her vehicle. She pulled into the ditch, Paige steering that way as well. When they were off the road, Erin braked all the way, bringing both of the vehicles to a stop.

Paige took her hands off the steering wheel. They were visibly shaking. She was breathing fast and hard. Jesse didn't want her to hyperventilate.

"Paige," he said firmly, "look at me."

She peeled her gaze away from the windshield. Her amazing pale blue eyes latched on to his. They were widened with fear. Her dark lashes whispered against her pale skin as she blinked at him.

"You did great," he said. Her hands were still trembling, so he grabbed them in his own. "We're safe now. We're safe. Okay?"

She nodded slowly. Then she closed her eyes, pulled in a deep breath and blew it out.

Her eyes flew open, and she twisted around in her seat. "Molly!"

"She's all right," Jesse said.

Erin knocked on his window, grabbing his attention. He opened the door.

"Everyone all right in here?" she asked.

"Yes. You're a lifesaver. Literally," he said.

"Damage to the vehicles is minimal." She blew out a breath. "Not that the vehicles matter. I tried hard to match your speed so the impact wouldn't be too bad."

"You did great," Jesse said. He didn't point out that if Erin hadn't been in front of them, if she hadn't answered her phone, the outcome would have been very different.

"Do you mind if I get Molly and the booster seat?" Erin asked.

"Please," Paige agreed, her voice quaking.

When she and Jesse were alone in the car, she pressed her hands against her face. Jesse suspected Erin had likely taken Molly because she knew Paige needed a moment to pull herself together.

"You okay?" he asked gently.

Her hands slid away from her face, and she turned to him, her eyes watery as she blinked back tears.

"Why would they do this?" Paige lamented. "The man in the woods said they didn't want to hurt Molly! Why would they put her at risk like this?"

"I don't think these men are too bright," Jesse said. "Unfortunately, that doesn't make them any less dangerous. In fact, it might make them more dangerous, because they act foolishly. I wonder if they figured Molly survived one accident being in the booster seat, maybe she'd survive another."

"Or maybe," Paige murmured, "they are so desperate to get rid of me, they just don't care."

Yeah, Jesse thought, there was always that possibility.

He realized that after leaving the boat landing, the men must've looped back to the campground, cut the brake lines and taken off again. Because they were dealing with something as serious as an attempted shooting, Deputy Harris had stopped to pick up the sheriff before heading to the campground, likely giving the criminals just enough time to backtrack and then flee.

"I'm going to give Gloria a call," he said. "I doubt she's gone too far. How about you go check on Molly?" He knew the child was all right physically, but he had to imagine that she would be affected by the events of the day.

She nodded, fumbled with the door handle and clambered out of the car.

He put in a call to the sheriff first, followed by a call

to the tow-truck company. Chad was tied up with the boat, just as Jesse had assumed, but Gloria assured him she was on her way. She'd sit with the car until a tow truck came. Then the car would be inspected. Jesse was sure they'd confirm it had been tampered with.

While he made the calls, Erin helped Paige transfer all of their bags into the SUV. Jesse kept watch all the while, not convinced the men wouldn't come back. He had everyone pile into Erin's vehicle, where they could wait with the heater on.

When Gloria arrived, she pulled in behind Paige's car. He walked over to greet her.

She shook her head as she got out of her cruiser. "Looks like trouble just keeps finding you today."

"Sure does," Jesse agreed. "The tow truck is about twenty minutes out. We can wait with you until it gets here."

She gave him a look.

"What?" he grumbled.

"You're off duty." She gave him a solid pat on the back. "Vacation. Remember?"

He frowned.

She shook her head. "I mean, unless you think you need to stick around because you don't think I'm capable."

Oh, yes. He heard the humor in her voice, but it was also laced with a challenge.

"You're perfectly capable," he said and meant it.

"Look, I know you want to be kept in the loop. I'll make sure you are. But we both know the tow-truck driver isn't going to tell us anything. His job is simply to transport the vehicle, not inspect it."

She had a point.

"Go," she ordered. "You need to get that pair back to Erin's and get them settled in. They've had quite the time of it lately."

"You'll let me know if you hear anything about the car? Or the men?" he pressed.

"You know I will." She grinned. "And if I happen to forget, I know you know the number for the station. And my cell. And Chad's cell."

"Right," he said, feeling more amused than annoyed thanks to her gentle chastising.

He thanked her, then strode back toward the SUV. He couldn't stop himself from glancing over his shoulder. She shook her head at him and gave him a stern look. He got the point. She had things handled here on the side of the road. It was his job to take care of the precious cargo inside his sister's vehicle.

Paige was entirely content with her one-story pale yellow house complete with white shutters and white picket fence, but that didn't stop the wave of admiration she felt when they pulled up in front of Erin's home.

The big, modern farmhouse looked inviting with its white siding and red front door. A wrought iron outdoor dining set adorned the wraparound porch. Vibrant crimson flowers dangled from pots at each side of the steps.

A large, brightly painted red barn was off to the side with plenty of fenced-in pasture. Erin had mentioned she'd turned her ranch into an animal rescue, of sorts. She took in animals in need that she ran across due to her career as a vet. She had an office in town, but this time of year, she spent a lot of time driving to farms, checking on livestock, which was her specialty.

There was a corral with a white wooden fence right

off the barn. Inside, a mare lazily flicked her tail as her foal trotted around. There were perhaps half a dozen more horses in the pasture. A gray tabby cat darted off the porch, her belly jiggling as she trotted across the driveway to disappear behind the barn, and a flock of rust-colored chickens scattered at the disturbance. A large German shepherd stood sentinel over it all.

Molly's eyes were glued to the horses in the field. The next few days, maybe even weeks, were bound to be stressful. Assuming she and Molly stayed here, the animals could be a good distraction for her niece.

"Are you hungry?" Erin asked.

Paige was absolutely ravenous. "I could eat." Her nerves had been frazzled at breakfast, and she'd barely touched her oatmeal. In the melee, they'd skipped lunch. And after an escape across the lake, a trek through the woods and a dip in frigid water, she was famished.

"I have some leftover enchiladas I can warm up," Erin said. "I'll get dinner started, and Jesse can show you to your rooms."

They slid from the SUV, and the dog trotted up to them. He went straight to Molly, who shrank away from him. To Paige's relief, Jesse stepped between them and knelt down, gently tugging the dog's collar to keep him in place.

"Molly," he said, "this is Gus. He wants to be everyone's best friend. Do you like dogs?"

She stared at Gus wide-eyed and shrugged. The dog was nearly as tall as she was. Paige didn't blame her for feeling intimidated.

Tentatively, Molly lifted her hand to pet the dog. He leaned into her touch, eyes closing, tongue lolling.

"He won't hurt you," Jesse said. "Is it okay if I let go of his collar?"

Molly nodded. The dog stayed put, soaking up the girl's attention. Paige gave Gus a gentle rub along his spine, and he looked at her adoringly.

"Old Gus here is the reason Erin decided to become a vet," he said as he hoisted his duffel bag over one shoulder and then grabbed Molly's bag. Paige reached into the back of the SUV for her own. "He showed up one morning her senior year of high school. He was emaciated, covered in ticks, was kind of roughed up, like maybe he'd gotten into an argument with a raccoon. He was skittish as could be, but she won him over, nursed him back to health and decided that's what she wanted to do with her life."

"So this is a family ranch?" Paige asked.

They started toward the house with Gus and Molly a step behind.

"Sure is," he said.

"It's huge," Paige replied, her admiration showing. "She lives here all alone?"

He chuckled. "For the moment, yes. It works out perfectly for us. However, she recently reconnected with Felix Jameson, her high school sweetheart. Now that they're both settled in their careers, I guess they figure it's time to focus on each other."

"Will she tell him I'm here?" Paige asked.

"Not if I ask her not to. She'll keep it quiet until this is all over. Felix is a good guy. I trust him completely, but I think the fewer people who know you're here, the better," Jesse said.

After their bags had been carried inside, Jesse pulled a camping cot from storage, took sheets out of the linen closet and set up a bed for Molly in the same room as Paige. Their room was down the hallway on the second floor, right across from Erin's. Jesse explained he'd be sleeping on the pullout sofa downstairs in the den. Closer to the front door.

Paige was grateful for his vigilance. She tried telling herself she would be safe here. She *should* be safe here. But she'd thought she was safe in her home, in the cabin, in her own car. And she hadn't been.

She ushered Molly into the bathroom across from their bedroom so they could wash up for dinner. As they descended the stairs, Paige's stomach roared. Molly looked at her with a hint of humor in her eyes.

Paige grinned at her niece, so relieved to see the lighthearted look. "I'm starving," she whispered. "I know you have to be, too."

The girl nodded, though she had snacked on cheese and crackers back at the cabin while Paige was being questioned.

"It smells delicious," Paige said as they entered the kitchen. She glanced around. "Looks like I'm a little late, but is there anything I can help with?"

Jesse shot her a quick smile. "We've got it covered. You two have a seat."

The table had been set. There was a pitcher of iced tea and a big bowl of cut-up melon. Jesse settled the casserole dish on the trivet in the center, and Erin placed a bowl of corn next to it. They dished up, said grace and enjoyed a few quiet moments of companionable silence while they all eased the worst of their hunger.

Finally, Erin said, "You and Molly look so much alike it's almost uncanny."

Paige smiled at Molly. The family resemblance was

obvious. Paige and Lydia could have passed for twins at times, so it was no wonder that Molly resembled Paige.

"I'll take that as a compliment," Paige said, winking at Molly.

Molly's lips twitched as she stabbed at another piece of melon.

"It's funny how that works in families," Paige said. "You and Jesse don't look anything alike."

Jesse was the epitome of tall, dark and handsome. Erin was fair skinned, green eyed, with a halo of blond curls.

Jesse and Erin shared an amused look.

"We're not related," he admitted with a shrug. "Not by blood, I mean."

Paige's brow furrowed. He'd referred to Erin as his sister. She was sure of it. "I thought you were siblings?" Had he meant half siblings? Stepsiblings?

"Technically, Erin is my foster sister," Jesse said, his tone light.

Erin nodded. "Jesse came to live with us when he was thirteen. I was in my senior year of high school, getting ready to head off to college."

"Oh," Paige said, her stomach dipping. She hoped she hadn't inadvertently brought up a stressful topic.

"He was such a charmer, my parents couldn't turn him away," Erin said with a twinkle in her eye, allaying Paige's concern.

"What she means," Jesse said wryly, "is that I was such a terror, no other family would take me."

"Okay. Yes, that's what I meant. But it's better coming out of your mouth than mine." Erin laughed. "Once I left for college, I still came home on weekends. It only took about a decade, but the kid finally grew on me."

Jesse quirked an eyebrow at her.

Her amusement lit up her face. "Fine. It wasn't that long. But he was a handful for the first several years. Eventually, he wised up and straightened out. Obviously."

"Because your parents never gave up on me," Jesse said.

"That," Erin said, giving Paige a knowing smile, "and because he got hooked on Mom's cooking."

Now Jesse laughed. "She is a great cook."

"You must have learned from her," Paige said.

Erin beamed.

They finished off the rest of the meal while making small talk. No one wanted to take on a heavy topic with Molly at the table.

"I'll wash dishes," Paige said. "It's the least I can do."

Erin looked like she was about to protest, but Paige saw Jesse give Erin a subtle nod.

"Sure," Erin said with a bright smile. "I'd be grateful. I have animals to tend to."

"I'll help with the dishes," Jesse said.

Erin leaned forward, her attention on Molly. "Now that you've made friends with Gus, would you like to meet a puppy?"

Molly hesitated, her eyes darting to Paige, who gave her an encouraging smile.

"I've got the cutest little pup I'd like you to meet," Erin said. "She's an orphan, and she's too small to be out in the barn alone. I keep her in a playpen just down the hallway. We don't have to go far."

Molly bit her lip, her curiosity clearly piqued.

"She's still so small she needs to drink out of a bottle," Erin continued. "She needs extra-special care. The very best thing in the world for her is extra love and snuggles. Do you think you could help me with that?"

"I think Molly would be an excellent helper," Paige said. She knew what Erin was doing. The woman was trying to give her and Jesse some time to talk, to dig into this mess without little ears overhearing.

Molly slid from her chair, following Erin out of the room.

I guess that's an affirmative, Paige thought. She wondered if her niece would ever speak again. They'd had a brief meeting with a child psychologist before leaving the hospital. The woman had told Paige that Molly's condition had been brought on by losing her mother in such a traumatic way. She had assured Paige that Molly should make a full recovery with time. She had also given Paige the name of a therapist in Grand Junction and encouraged her to get Molly in right away.

That was one more way she'd failed her niece. They'd taken off before she'd had a chance to make an appointment. She hoped the delay wouldn't cause any lasting effects.

"You look lost in thought," Jesse said.

She shook herself back to reality. "I'm just thinking. About Molly," she clarified. "I'm worried about her. I'm worried she'll never talk again."

"Give it time," Jesse encouraged. "Her mother's death is still pretty recent."

Paige winced, then nodded. "You're right. But I'm worried about today. How is she supposed to heal from trauma when I can't keep her safe?"

"I get what you're saying. Molly's safety should be our number one priority."

"Our?" Paige asked. "You just met us. I can't believe—"

"Going after bad guys is what I do," Jesse said, keeping his tone light. Yet Paige knew that what he was doing went above and beyond. "Let's get these dishes done. Then I'd like to ask a few more questions. It'll take them a while to mix the bottle and feed the puppy, but I get the impression Molly isn't going to want to be away from you for long."

"You know," Jesse said as he handed a dish to Paige to dry, "it works in our favor at the moment that Erin isn't a blood relation. If those goons took the registration off my boat—which, frankly, I'm not convinced they were smart enough to do—there's really no way for them to trace me to Erin or this ranch." He was convinced the men hadn't seen Erin pick them up at the lake. They must have been too busy cutting Paige's brake lines. And there hadn't been another vehicle on the return trip to the campground. "I never took the Coopers' last name, even though I consider them family."

"Where are they now? The Coopers?" Paige asked.

"Hank and Ellen? They handed the ranch over to Erin when she started her vet practice two years ago. Now they winter in Florida," he said. "They spend most of the year there. There's a renovated loft apartment over the barn. When they come back in the summer, they stay there."

"Do you live nearby?" Paige asked.

"Not far. I have a small cabin on five acres at the edge of town. I hope to get something with a little more land someday. But right now, it's just me." He shrugged. "So it's all I need."

"It sounds nice," she said. "I live in town, and while

I like my neighbors, sometimes I think a bit of privacy would be nice."

"Can't argue that." Jesse rinsed another plate and handed it off. "What else can you tell me about your sister and her marriage? After what happened today, and the other events you told me about, I'm willing to explore the possibility that there was foul play in her death. However, I think we need to keep an open mind."

"Is there anything in particular that you want to know?"

"I'd like to know more about Lydia," he said gently. "I know you said there was a rift between the two of you, but tell me what you can."

"Growing up, we were really close. I was only a year older. A few years ago, Lydia and I had a falling-out," Paige said as she slid a glass into the cupboard. "I knew she didn't love Abe, and I told her she shouldn't marry him. I told her Molly deserved better. She accused me of thinking she was a bad mother." She pulled in a shaky breath. "That's not what I meant. I simply meant Molly deserved to have parents who loved each other. But she was furious." She gave a helpless shrug. "That's the condensed version. There were many discussions and borderline arguments leading up to our big fight. She and Abe eloped, got married in the Bahamas. She cut off communication with me shortly after that."

That caught Jesse's interest. "Why did she marry a man she didn't love? Was she after his money?"

Paige winced. "You might look at it that way. But I know my sister. She was after *stability*."

The dishes were done now. Jesse pulled the plug, allowing the water to swirl down the drain, and they leaned against the counter, facing each other.

"Stability?" he pressed.

"To understand what I mean, I need to back up," Paige said. "Lydia married her high school sweetheart, Tom, just a few months after graduation. They had Molly a little more than a year later. They were in love, head over heels, but money was tight. They were young. Neither of them had a good job. Lydia waited tables at a diner. Tom worked the night shift at a factory. I already mentioned he was killed on his way to work. After that, Lydia really struggled. She and Molly moved in with me for a while."

"You mentioned he died when Molly was an infant," Jesse stated.

She nodded. "My sister struggled with depression for a while. She just couldn't get on her feet. She enrolled in a local university, but between her grief, being a mother, studying for classes and still needing to work," Paige said, looking crushed, "it was just too much for her. She dropped out of school and got a job waitressing at the country club in the evenings, when I could watch Molly. That's where she met Abe."

Paige explained that her sister was tired of struggling. She was young, beautiful, and she pursued Abe almost relentlessly. He was older, divorced, not particularly attractive. He ate up the attention. Lydia had told Paige she'd married for love once, and it hurt too much to even think about doing that again. She didn't want to remain single forever. She craved a relationship where someone would take care of her.

Abe could provide that.

They were married within the year.

Jesse was quiet, absorbing everything Paige had shared.

"I know how it sounds," she said. "But for my sister, it was a matter of self-preservation, not selfishness. I'm sure Abe knew where she stood. She was able to quit her job, become a housewife. She—"

"She was a trophy wife," Jesse said bluntly.

Paige winced but nodded.

"You think Abe knew she didn't love him?" Jesse asked.

"I assumed," she said, "but looking back, I have no idea."

"Whether he did or didn't," he said, "having a wife who doesn't love you typically doesn't lead to murder."

They had no real motive, and that needled Jesse. Before Paige could respond, his phone chimed. He glanced at the screen and then immediately answered. He listened to everything Sheriff Sanchez had to say and wasn't at all surprised by the news she shared. When he hung up, he turned to Paige, who was eyeing him with wariness.

"We just got confirmation," Jesse said. "Your brake lines were definitely cut."

Paige pressed her hand to her mouth and turned away from him. She didn't look surprised, only scared.

He didn't blame her.

If these men were determined enough to track Paige down at a campground, shoot at her *and* cut her brake lines, they probably weren't going to stop there. He was afraid this wasn't over. Not even close.

FIVE

The next morning, Jesse stepped out of the den, not surprised to hear Erin rattling around in the kitchen already. What did surprise him was spotting Molly sitting at the bottom of the staircase with Gus at her feet. Paige must be sleeping pretty soundly if Molly had managed to slip away. He knew she'd had a few stressful weeks and figured she probably hadn't slept much since her sister's death. He was glad she felt comfortable enough to get some rest now.

He'd slept okay since he knew Gus would alert them to a stranger in a heartbeat. He trusted the dog's instincts implicitly. No one would get close to the house without Gus barking out a warning.

"Did you sleep well?" Jesse asked. Was that even a legitimate question for a kid? Didn't they all hate bedtime or something?

Molly nodded, and he felt a bit better about asking.

"Is Paige still sleeping?"

Another nod, but she remained planted on the bottom step. They still had a few hours before Paige's appointment with Mr. Zielinski, the lawyer.

"Are you hungry?"

She slid off the steps, landing on her feet.

"What would you like for breakfast?" he asked.

She turned her head away. He knew it wouldn't be that easy to get her to speak, but it wouldn't hurt to try.

"I like waffles," Jesse said as Molly followed him into the kitchen. Gus, knowing it was the one room of the house he wasn't allowed in, dropped down in the doorway with a pitiful groan. "And pancakes. I guess I really like omelets, too," he said. "In other words, I'm not picky."

"That's fortunate," Erin said, "because I'm not making any of those. I'm putting together an egg bake."

"Need some help?" he asked. Molly climbed onto the edge of a stool, and her gaze swung between them.

"I wouldn't turn it down," Erin said. "You can either take over with breakfast or feed the puppy. I got up around two, but she's bound to be hungry again."

"I can do that," Jesse said. He was about to head down the hallway that led to the laundry room off the mudroom when Erin called his name.

He pivoted, shooting her a questioning look.

She nodded toward Molly. The girl was staring at him.

Huh. "Wanna come with me?" he asked.

She leaped off the stool.

"I'll take that as a yes," he said with a chuckle.

They made their way to the laundry room, where Erin had set up a playpen for the puppy. She was far too small to have free run of the house. She stirred when she heard footsteps, and by the time they reached the playpen, the puppy was sitting on her haunches, whimpering for attention. The stuffed animal Erin had purchased, with an electronic beating heart to comfort her, lay forgotten.

"Hey, little one," Jesse said. He reached inside, scooped up the animal and hugged her close to his chest. He'd been the one to bring her to Erin, and he felt a connection to the pup. She'd grown since he'd rescued her at only a few weeks old. Still, the wriggly creature barely weighed a few pounds. Erin figured she was around five weeks old now, and she had been able to start her on some soft food recently, which helped immensely with cutting down bottle feedings.

Molly settled into one of the camp chairs Erin had set up in here for just this purpose.

"Do you want to feed her again?" he asked.

Molly nodded and reached for the puppy.

He'd prepared the pup's bottle a time or two before, so he prepped it quickly.

He knelt beside her and placed the squirming bundle on her lap, then handed her the bottle. Like a pro, she popped it in the puppy's mouth while the pup sat in her lap. Jesse kept a hand on the puppy's back to keep her from getting excited and toppling off.

Molly's face was rapturous as she watched the tiny predominantly white dog with brown patches. She had brown markings covering most of her face, and her big dark eyes peered out at them. She made silly slurpy noises as she drank. Milk dribbled down her chin, and Jesse dabbed at it with a napkin Erin had left there.

Molly giggled quietly. Jesse thought it was the sweetest sound he'd ever heard. He studied her for a moment, unable to help himself from wondering what she'd seen. Could it be that Molly knew what had happened the night her mother was killed? If only she would talk. He wouldn't think of questioning her without Paige present, but he definitely wondered what she knew. The sooner they could get her talking, the sooner they may get some answers.

"We need to find a name for this little gal," Jesse said, hoping to land on a topic that would grab her interest. Erin didn't typically name her rescue animals, saving that honor for their adoptive families, but this might be a good time to make an exception. "Maybe you could help me out. Do you think you could?"

She nodded, looking uncertain.

"How about—" he scratched his chin "—Lucille?"

She shook her head.

"Spot?"

Another negative.

"Huh." He scratched the puppy's head. "Peanut?"

She scrunched up her face, looking disappointed in his suggestions.

"I'll take that as another no," he said.

"What in the world are you two talking about?" Paige asked as she appeared in the doorway.

Jesse gave Molly a conspiratorial look. "Do you want to tell her, or should I?"

She pointed at him, and he chuckled, because of course he'd known that would be her answer.

"Little puppy here doesn't have a name," Jesse explained. "Molly and I are not doing a very good job of figuring it out."

"Oh, my. She's precious," Paige crooned as she sidled up beside them.

Jesse had been so intent on Molly and the puppy that he hadn't heard her approach. She looked refreshed. Her face was scrubbed clean, and her dark hair was pulled back in a tidy ponytail. She knelt down beside them.

"She's so tiny. What breed is she?" Paige asked.

"Erin thinks there's maybe a bit of Chihuahua, a smidge of terrier, but for the most part, she's beagle."

"She's darling," Paige declared.

Jesse wanted to ask Paige if she'd like to keep her. Erin would be looking for a home for her soon. But given how smitten Molly was with the pup, he knew better than to put Paige on the spot like that.

"Molly," Paige said, "it looks like you found a little buddy."

The girl smiled, *actually smiled*, and nodded.

Paige beamed back at her and then turned to Jesse. "How is it she doesn't have a name yet?"

"Erin takes care of a lot of strays. She feels it should be up to the new owners to choose the name, so as not to confuse the animal if they decide to change it." Jesse leaned in, his tone confiding. "If you ask me, I think naming them makes her feel too attached. If she had room, she'd keep every one. But it's just not feasible."

Paige arched a brow. "Yet you think you need to name this little one?"

He nodded toward an entranced Molly. "It's an extenuating circumstance."

The puppy's head began to droop. The bottle was almost empty, and the puppy was wiped out from her efforts. She yawned and then curled up in Molly's lap.

"Do you want to hold her for a little while longer?" Jesse asked, taking the bottle.

Molly's nod was firm.

"How about we go into the living room? It's kind of boring in here with nothing to look at but the washer and dryer." He carefully scooped Molly into his arms, careful not to dislodge the sleeping puppy. The little girl looked happy. He realized it was the first time she'd looked truly happy since he'd met her.

He carried her to the living room, Paige hustling ahead of him. Last night, she'd put in one of Molly's movies for her. She turned it on now. A cartoon cocker spaniel and a mutt popped up on the screen. Jesse settled Molly on the couch, the pup still snuggled in her lap.

"We're going to see if Erin needs help with breakfast," Paige told Molly. "Just come find me if you need something. Okay?"

The child's head bobbed, but she was barely paying attention to Paige or the TV. She was raptly watching the sleeping puppy in her lap. She petted her with soft, gentle strokes. Paige and Jesse shared a smile as they headed toward the kitchen.

"Breakfast will be done in about ten minutes," Erin said, checking her watch. "Then I better head out. I have a full day ahead of me." She paused, her gaze resting on Paige. "You know, I'm going to the Bernard farm today. I'll be spending the entire morning inoculating their new calves. Would it be all right if I brought Molly with me? MaryAnn is a high school friend. She's got four-year-old twin daughters. I'm sure Molly would enjoy playing with them."

Paige winced. "I couldn't impose like that."

"You're not imposing," Erin said. She gave Paige a guilty smile. "In fact, I called MaryAnn last night to see if it would be all right. I hope I didn't overstep, but I knew you planned on going to the lawyer's office today."

Jesse and Erin had talked about it last night after

Paige went to bed. When Erin mentioned bringing Molly with her, he'd been grateful. He planned on digging into this case but was worried Molly's presence would hinder his investigation.

"We don't know what we're going to find out at the lawyer's office," Jesse said. "It's probably not the best place to bring Molly. She might overhear something disturbing. Or the lawyer might not feel comfortable talking with her there."

"I know you're right," Paige agreed, "but I don't like the idea of being away from her right now."

"Your first priority is to keep her safe," Jesse gently reminded her. "One of the safest places she could be today is on a ranch surrounded by cowboys. No one will get past that crew."

Paige seemed to mull it over for a few seconds. Then she agreed. "I better go tell her."

Jesse watched her go, and when his gaze swung back around, Erin was shaking her head at him.

"You're on vacation," she reminded him. "And you're going to spend all your time looking into a case. Why am I not surprised?"

He didn't bother to respond.

"Tell me why you went to the Hideaway," she pressed. "It's barely fifteen minutes out of town. We live in a beautiful state with probably hundreds of getaways."

He shrugged. "Yeah, dozens of places just like the Hideaway. So why travel for hours when I didn't have to?"

"You say you might want to leave the department," Erin said. "But I think you stayed close because you didn't want to miss out on any excitement. You wanted

to be nearby in case something came up and the department needed you."

Jesse's lips twisted.

"I know I'm right." She sighed. "Don't let that whole
mess with Trish get into your head. You're good at what
you do. You're definitely dedicated. Not a soul would
argue with that."

Jesse grimaced, because he didn't want to think
about Trish. She was a con woman at best, a thief at
worst. Though he wasn't sure she'd ever gotten her
hands dirty. No. She'd just been the informant for a
theft ring that had spent the winter breaking into the
fancy, deserted summer lake homes. Tens of thousands
of dollars' worth of electronics, jewelry and artwork had
been stolen. Thankfully, he hadn't given up any information he shouldn't have, had never violated protocol
when she'd so innocently asked about the cases. But he
had given up his heart. And in the end, she'd shredded
it, bled his emotions dry.

He'd thought he was falling for her. She'd come
across as so sweet, caring, attentive, but it was all a
ploy. One night, when they were having a late-night
date around a campfire at his house, he'd gotten an
emergency call to help with a break-in. He'd taken off,
leaving Trish to put out the fire because she'd offered.
But he'd realized he'd forgotten his phone in his camp
chair and rushed back to get it. Trish hadn't heard his
approach, but he'd heard her. She'd been on the phone
telling someone to clear out. That cops were on the way,
so they needed to move fast.

In the end, it was a blessing he'd overheard the call.
It was through Trish that they'd ended up tracking down
the thieves.

Last fall, she'd had a flat tire just a few miles from his home. He found out later she'd scoped him out, learned his routine. She'd timed it so that she was stranded on the side of the road as he was coming home from work in the wee hours of the morning. She claimed she'd been out for a drive after suffering from a bout of insomnia.

Liar.

She'd been a liar. And he'd been a fool to buy into her tale. While he'd technically done nothing wrong, it annoyed him to no end that he'd been duped. It had made him second-guess himself and his career choice. He'd tried handing in his resignation last week, but the sheriff had simply shaken her head and told him to take a vacation instead.

He had no desire to go through an ordeal like that again. Although, he had to admit, he knew what was happening with Paige was no charade. The gunfire had been about as real as real could get.

Paige returned to the kitchen and smiled at him, and he forced one back, reminding himself that he didn't know her at all. He'd help her out, hopefully solve this case and then send her and Molly on their way.

He wasn't going to let another woman tug at his heart and yank it out of his chest. Not again.

Rodney Zielinski ran his law practice out of an old house on a downtown street on the edge of Cascade Falls. It was far from fancy, but Paige thought maybe that helped his clients feel at ease.

"It's a few minutes to ten," Jesse said. "We should get in there." He'd been all business since breakfast.

She momentarily wondered if she'd done something

wrong, but she tried to assure herself he was just taking this upcoming visit seriously.

She reached for her door handle, pushed the door open and slid into the cool, brisk morning air. They walked up the sidewalk together, and she noticed that he scanned the street, looking over his shoulder before they knocked on the door.

"Do you think we were followed?" she asked, a shiver of fear slowly creeping down her spine.

"What I think," he replied, "is that we can't be too careful. I don't think anyone knows we're at the ranch. I don't see how they possibly could. But this office is the type of place I'd stake out if I were a criminal. I think it's likely they tracked you with your phone's GPS. If they managed to listen in on your calls, they'll know you plan on showing up here."

Paige looked up and down the street, the tingling along her spine intensifying. Were they being watched? Spied on? *Hunted?* It was an eerie, terrifying thought. The man in the woods had said he didn't want to hurt Molly. Though he'd clearly wanted Paige dead, and she couldn't help but assume he wouldn't think twice about hurting Jesse to get to her. The thought made dread spill through her veins.

Jesse pushed the door open, causing a bell above them to jingle. He motioned for her to go in first. Then he quickly stepped inside.

Plush beige carpeting covered the floor. The walls were cream, and wildlife photos hung neatly around the area. Off to the left, in what must have been a sitting room at one time, sat a leather sofa, two chairs and a coffee table covered with magazines for waiting clients to peruse.

A wiry woman with an abundance of wrinkles and unnaturally red hair glanced up at them. She flashed a welcoming smile.

"What can I help you with?" she asked.

"I had an appointment with Mr. Zielinski today at ten," Paige said.

"Oh dear." The woman's smile slipped into a frown. She tapped her keyboard. "Paige Bennett?"

"Yes," Paige said.

"Mr. Zielinski had to cancel all of his appointments for today," the woman explained. "I contacted everyone on his calendar. I have a note by your name. I'm Bernadette. I left a voice mail for you. Didn't you receive it?"

"I broke my phone," Paige said with a grimace. If waterlogged and shorted out counted as broken, it was about as broken as could be. "I didn't get the message. Are you saying he won't be in at all today?"

"No, he won't be," Bernadette said apologetically.

Jesse stepped forward. "How soon can we reschedule? We have an urgent matter we need to discuss with him."

"I'm not sure," Bernadette admitted. "Is there something I can help you with?"

Paige glanced at Jesse. He gave her an encouraging nod.

"I spoke to Mr. Zielinski yesterday. He was doing some work for my sister, Lydia Winslow. He agreed to meet with me today to discuss her will," Paige explained.

"I'm sorry. I wish I had better news for you."

"I don't suppose you could give me his number?" Jesse pressed.

Bernadette frowned. "I can't do that."

Jesse slid his wallet out of his pocket. He flashed his badge at Bernadette. "I'm with the Cascade Falls Sheriff's Department. Lydia Winslow was killed in a car accident, and we need to eliminate foul play. She recently had Mr. Zielinski draw up her will. We need to question him. It's imperative that we find out if Lydia shared any information with him."

"Are you really with the sheriff's department?" Bernadette asked, sounding almost relieved.

Jesse held out the badge again, letting her study it this time. "You can call in and ask, if you'd like, but yes, I am."

"The truth is, I'm worried about Rodney," Bernadette said, her voice strained.

Jesse and Paige shared startled glances.

"Why is that?" Jesse asked.

"He rarely misses a day of work," Bernadette said. "His wife died a little over a year ago. Ovarian cancer hit fast and hard. Now he even comes in on the weekend to fill up his time. So it's strange that he took today off when he had a full schedule. Stranger still, he texted me that he wasn't coming in."

"That's unusual?" Jesse asked.

She nodded. "I didn't know he even knew how to text."

The chill Paige had felt on the front steps was back, skating slowly up and down her spine, skittering down her arms, sliding down her legs. Her knees were weak, and fear began to pool in the pit of her stomach. She did not like where this conversation was going.

"There's something else," Bernadette admitted. She wrung her hands together, as if building up the courage to speak. "I'm sure it's nothing, and I hate to imply that Mr. Zielinski is absentminded, because I assure you, he is not."

"But?" Jesse pressed.

She frowned. "It's not unusual for him to come in on the weekends. As you said, he was here yesterday. The odd thing is, not only did he forget to lock the front door, but it was open a crack," she admitted. "And the alarm wasn't set."

"That's unusual?" Paige asked, her voice calm, despite her rising panic.

"The door being open, yes, but he's not always very good about the alarm. He installed it because he thought it would bring his clients a level of comfort to know their information is secure. But truth be told, when it was first installed, he accidentally set it off one too many times. He more or less gave up on it, hoping the logo of the security company attached to the doors would be deterrent enough." Her eyes darted between them. "But to leave the door open *and* unlocked? Pair that with *texting* and not coming in to work, and, well, I'm not sure what to make of his unusual behavior. I tried calling him, but he didn't answer. I thought about having an officer drive by his house, but I didn't want to overstep. If he's fine, I don't think he'd appreciate my meddling." She paused. "But he's been so distraught since his wife's passing. Simply not himself."

"Are you worried about his mental state?" Jesse asked carefully.

She bit her lip, nodded, then said, "He's sharp as a tack, mind you. It's not that. But he's been, well… He's been depressed. And now this."

"I'd be happy to drive by his house," Jesse said. "If you give me his address."

"I'd be grateful." Bernadette clicked away at her keyboard again. Then she grabbed a sticky note and a pen. She scribbled down his address and handed it to Jesse.

"I have a quick favor to ask in return," Jesse said. "Can you let us see Lydia Winslow's file?"

"Oh, I'm sorry. I can't do that. Mr. Zielinski's work is confidential," she said.

Paige stepped forward.

"I think this might change things." Paige pulled out a long cream-colored envelope with the law office's address stamped in the corner. "Mr. Zielinski, as I said, drew up her will. As you can see, this states that I'm the executor. I'm just wondering if he would have notes of any kind."

Bernadette took the papers from Paige and scanned them. She hesitated, pursing her lips, clearly trying to weigh her options.

"I'm the executor," Paige pressed. "I believe that gives me the right to ask you a few questions about the work Mr. Zielinski did."

The older woman hefted out a resigned sigh. She returned to her keyboard. Paige shifted from foot to foot worriedly when a crease formed between the older woman's brows.

"Lydia *Winslow*?" Bernadette finally tried to clarify.

"Yes," Paige said.

Bernadette shook her head. "I'm sorry. We keep files by last name, and I'm not finding her."

"Try Bennett," Jesse suggested. "It was her maiden name, right?"

Paige nodded her agreement, though she knew that her sister had not used her maiden name on any of the paperwork that was sent to Paige.

"I'm sorry," Bernadette said again. "I'm not find-ing that either." She held out her hand. "May I see your paperwork again?"

Paige obligingly handed over her sister's will.

"This just simply does not make sense," Bernadette said. "This is dated from the last month. She should be in our system. Rodney and I use a shared drive, so I should have access to everything. It's a standard will." She tapped a contemplative finger against her desk, then stood. "Nearly a decade ago, we had a computer issue that resulted in lost files. Since then, Rodney has always kept paper copies as backup. He also files any notes instead of taking the time to scan them all in. Let me check his file cabinet."

She padded down the hallway and disappeared.

"I don't like this," Jesse said. "It's awfully suspicious timing for him to start behaving erratically. Do you re-member what time you spoke with him yesterday?"

"I don't remember exactly," Paige said, "but it was right after breakfast. He was pleasant when we spoke."

"Barely twenty-four hours ago," Jesse said.

They both knew a lot could happen in twenty-four hours.

Bernadette shuffled back into the room. "There's no file on your sister. I thought maybe he misfiled it, so I sorted through the entire *W* section, even though he isn't prone to misfiling."

Somehow, Paige wasn't even surprised by the news.

"What could have happened to the file?" Jesse pressed.

"It's incredibly odd that both the electronic and paper copy are missing," Bernadette stated. "If I had to guess,

I'd say the electronic file was deleted, because it certainly existed a month ago."

Paige was afraid of that. She pulled a photo from her purse. It was an old wallet-sized photo, but Lydia hadn't changed much.

"This is my sister. Do you recognize her?" Paige asked.

Bernadette studied the picture, though distractedly. "I don't think I do."

Jesse took the photo from Paige. "Can I use the scanner?"

Bernadette nodded absently, her thoughts clearly on her employer and the missing files, not on the pair in front of her. Jesse made a copy of the picture and placed it on the woman's desk. "When things have settled down, take a good hard look. See if her face rattles any memories free."

Paige jotted her number down on a small sheet of notebook paper she pulled from her purse. "If you think of anything, please call me. I don't have a phone at the moment, but I hope to soon. If you leave a message, I'll call back."

Jesse added his number to the note. "For backup."

"You'll go check on Rodney now?" Bernadette asked.

"Yes," Jesse said. "Now we check on Rodney."

Rodney Zielinski's home was in a quiet, upscale neighborhood tucked back among the trees. The house was a tidy gray two-story with a covered porch. It was too early in the year to tell, but Paige suspected the flower beds would boast gorgeous blooms and the yard would be meticulously maintained.

Yet something about the house gave Paige an eerie feeling. Almost a sense of foreboding. She studied the place, and it only took her a moment to realize why. The curtains on the bottom floor were all tugged shut.

"It looks like he likes his privacy," she said wryly.

The house was skirted by trees, so pulling the curtains closed this time of day seemed odd. Was the lawyer trying to hide something? Was someone else trying to hide something? Paige hated to think so, but that was what she suspected.

"I hope that's all it is," Jesse muttered. He reached for the door handle. "Maybe you should stay in the truck. Lock the doors."

"No," Paige said. "I'm coming with you." It wasn't just that she was too involved, too invested, to be left behind. Truth be told, she felt safer by Jesse's side. Ironic, given that he could very well be walking into danger.

They got out of the truck, and Jesse motioned for her to get behind him. She complied, but not before noticing how his hand went to his holstered gun. She was relieved he had the weapon. Not because she hoped he'd use it, but because she hoped if they ran into trouble, the gun would be a deterrent.

He was hypervigilant as they made their way up the sidewalk. She heard him make a small sound of displeasure when they reached the front door.

"I don't like the looks of this." He glanced at her and gave the door a gentle nudge. It swung open a few more inches. "Mr. Zielinski?" He shouted the man's name while still on the other side of the threshold. She understood he couldn't barge into the man's home. That wouldn't do if everything happened to be okay.

Unfortunately, Paige had a feeling everything was *not* okay.

Jesse stabbed at the doorbell. Apparently, the apparatus was just inside the entry, right over their heads. Paige cringed at the raucous, reverberating sound.

"If that doesn't get his attention…" she muttered.

Jesse gave her an arched-eyebrow look as they waited a few more heartbeats.

"I'm going in," Jesse said. "I hate that we might have alerted anyone here, but I can't very well barge into a man's home just because his door is open a crack. With him not answering, and all of the suspicious activity," he said quietly, "I think entering is justified."

"Let's go," Paige whispered.

He held up a finger, indicating she should wait just a second, and then pushed the door open a bit wider. He stepped inside, looking to his left, his right, then back to his left. He nodded his head, and Paige stepped into the house, ready to follow him.

"I was going to do a sweep of the house," he whispered, "but I'm thinking maybe we should check that out first."

The kitchen was to the left of the entryway. There appeared to be another entry connected to it. The garage was on that end of the house, so it was safe to assume the door they could see led into the garage.

The partially *open* door.

Paige nodded her understanding.

Jesse drew his gun and quickly, quietly crossed the kitchen. Paige hurried behind him, glancing over her shoulder, lest they be ambushed from behind. When he reached the door, he peered into the garage, threw the door open and darted inside. It took Paige only a moment to realize why.

A white Cadillac was parked in the double-stall garage, a man slumped over the steering wheel. Jesse rushed to the car and tugged at the door. It was locked.

Bernadette had been worried about her boss's mental state. Had the man killed himself? How long had he been here? Since leaving the office yesterday? The car wasn't running, and she couldn't smell anything toxic. Had he shot himself? Overdosed? Thoughts whirled through her mind.

"Call for help." Jesse slammed his phone into her hand. As she started to dial, a squeak—the sort of squeak that sounded suspiciously like the sole of a shoe against concrete—caught their attention. In unison, they began to whirl around.

There was a blur of movement, and a wet and cloying rag was pressed over her face. She gasped in surprise, which only resulted in her sucking in the vapor. She tried to fight, to wiggle away, and could hear Jesse doing the same. A quick glimpse of the man attacking Jesse confirmed his attacker was wearing a black ski mask. She was unable to see her own attacker as he held her from behind. She tried to stomp on the man's foot, but her legs were like noodles. She heard a grunt that sounded like one of their attackers taking a punch. Her vision began to blur, and her awareness began to slip away. Her body became limp, her bones useless.

Then…nothing.

SIX

Paige groaned in agony as her eyelids fluttered. She coughed, gagged and tried to gather her wits. It took several precious moments for her to realize she was locked in Mr. Zielinski's garage. The fancy car hummed quietly as noxious fumes filled the small space. The moment she realized what was happening, she jerked herself upright.

Someone had drugged them, knocking them out, and now the lawyer's car was running, quickly filling the garage with deadly carbon monoxide.

"Jesse!" She gave his shoulder a hard shake. "Jesse! Wake up. Now!"

He began to stir, but she didn't have time to waste.

"Wake up!" she shouted again, this time while trying to scramble to her feet. The garage was already hazy with exhaust fumes. They burned her throat and made her eyes throb. She tugged her shirt over her mouth. Her head pounded, and she wasn't sure if it was from the carbon monoxide or whatever had been on that rag. It was probably a combination of the two.

Jesse stirred as Paige took a shaky step toward the garage door button.

"What…?" Jesse muttered as he stumbled to his feet. He seemed to assess their circumstances in a heartbeat. "We need to get out of here."

Paige was a step ahead of him. She slapped at the garage door button. The motor ran, gliding along the track, but the door didn't lift.

"They detached the arm that connects the door to the lift," Paige said.

Jesse, his face covered with his shirt as well, shuffled to the door that led back into the house. "Locked," he said, confirming what Paige already suspected. He glanced around, studying the floor. "They must've taken my phone." He paused, his expression hardening. "And my gun."

"There's no other way out," she said.

Jesse quickly crossed the garage, bent down and tried to slide his fingers under the big garage door, hoping to lift it up. It was leveled tightly against the floor, and he couldn't get any leverage. Paige noticed a piece of plywood nailed to the wall. She assumed that it covered a window. She went to it, pulled and, like Jesse with the door, couldn't get it to budge.

"We need to break into the car," Jesse said.

She whirled around, her head swimming as she scanned the area. Bile climbed her throat as acid seemed to slosh in her stomach.

"There're no tools in here," Jesse growled. "What kind of garage doesn't have tools?" He took off to inspect a nook tucked off the side of the entry into the house.

"Everything must be in the small gardening shed on the side of the garage," Paige said. He was right. The garage was immaculate, an organizer's dream. The back wall was lined with shelves. The shelves were lined with plastic totes all neatly labeled. They apparently held items such as holiday decorations and keepsakes, nothing that could help them break out of here.

Paige went back to the car, tried all four doors, though she knew it would be in vain. Fear made her fingers so shaky they were nearly useless. She tried not to look at the man crumpled in the front seat, her heart aching for him as she wondered about his family.

"Out of the way," Jesse ordered, his tone frantic, but not unkind. "I found something to use." He held up a golf club. "There's a set tucked in the back corner," he said as he hefted it behind him and swung. The window of the driver's-side back seat shattered, the cracks spiderwebbing out from a hole in the middle. He swung again. And again. Eventually, all the glass fell away. Wasting no time, he reached in and popped the locks. He gently pulled the lawyer from the front seat.

As Jesse carefully moved the man out of the way, Paige slid into the front seat. She tried not to think about the fact that she was sitting where a deceased man had been. Instead, she put her full concentration on the task at hand. She slammed the door closed, shifted into Reverse and stomped on the gas pedal.

The car shot backward. She flew forward in her seat, smashing into the steering wheel as the car crashed through the garage door. Belatedly, she realized a seat belt would've been wise, but time had been of the essence. Never mind that her brain was all fuzzy.

A sore chest would be worth it, because as she blinked and looked around, she realized she had accomplished what she'd set out to do. The sides of the big garage door had been torn off their tracks. The middle of the door was dented outward, and Paige could see into the yard along the sides.

Where there was fresh air.

She shut the car off, stopping the deadly fumes, and took a moment to gather herself.

Jesse tugged her door open, and she slipped out. Right into his arms.

"Great work," he murmured close to her ear.

"Thank God you found the club," she replied.

Fresh air was already swirling in, and the nauseating fumes were dissipating. Jesse released her and turned to the side of the garage, where the door had been torn away. The opening wasn't quite big enough to fit through, but with a hefty shove, he managed to slide the large door aside, creating an opening big enough for them to slide into the yard.

The untainted air filling their lungs and refreshing them was utterly blissful. Paige stood crouched over, hands on knees, sucking in the precious oxygen. When she managed a glance at Jesse, she realized he still clung to the golf club, and though he wasn't in top form, he was scanning the yard as if concerned the men would burst from the bushes. She admired his vigilance and didn't doubt he'd do his best to defend them, if need be.

When they had recovered enough to clear some of the haze from their minds, Jesse said, "I need to make a phone call."

After what felt like an interminable amount of time sitting in the back of an ambulance, breathing through an oxygen mask, Jesse and Paige finally recovered enough to be questioned. He told Sheriff Sanchez about the visit to Bernadette, finding Rodney Zielinski and the attack.

When they'd stumbled into the house to call 911, Jesse had spotted his cell phone, the screen smashed, in the kitchen sink. Along with his weapon. He was relieved his sidearm had been left behind, but the cell phone was a goner. These guys were smart enough to know not to be caught with an officer's weapon.

Despite the EMT crew encouraging them to go to the hospital, both Jesse and Paige adamantly declined. Not even Sheriff Sanchez could convince them otherwise, although she was so busy processing the crime scene, she didn't really push it.

Jesse and Paige were anxious to get back to the ranch, though they ended up making a few stops first. A quick conversation revealed they used the same cell phone carrier. Given the circumstances, he didn't want to be without.

Half an hour later, they walked out of the store with new phones. The sales attendant had given Paige an odd look when she'd requested a phone without GPS tracking, but he hadn't questioned her. He'd explained they only had one old flip phone in stock, and it was devoid of the GPS tracking module. Paige had not hesitated in choosing that one.

"How's the headache?" Jesse asked as they trudged across the parking lot to his truck. The men hadn't left evidence behind, but Jesse was sure they'd been drugged with chloroform. That, on top of the carbon monoxide, had left them both sluggish and nauseated, even after the treatment with an oxygen mask.

"Better," Paige said. "Yours?"

"I'm feeling better overall," he replied. "Not great, but definitely better."

Her footsteps slowed as they reached the truck. "I'd like to get back to the ranch," she said, "but I'm worried about Bernadette. She seemed to hold Mr. Zielinski in high regard. She worked for him a long time. She must be devastated. I'd like to check in on her."

"I was thinking the same thing," he admitted. While his concern for the woman was earnest, he also thought it couldn't hurt to touch base with her. "She may not still be there. If Deputy Harris is done speaking with her, she may have headed home. But it won't hurt to try."

The office was only a few minutes away. When they arrived, Chad's cruiser was still out front. So was a silver car he'd noticed earlier and assumed was Bernadette's. So the woman *was* still here.

Jesse knocked on the door, and Bernadette answered a moment later. The woman's eyes were red and watery. Faded mascara streaked across her face. She dabbed at her nose with a tissue.

"I was so relieved to hear you two are all right," she said. She stepped back and quickly ushered them inside. "I can't believe…" She seemed to strangle on a sob. "I can't believe he's gone. He was such a kind, gentle man."

"We are so very sorry for your loss," Jesse said and meant it.

Bernadette nodded. "At least he's with Ethel again. I have to remember that. I know he's in a better place."

"Does he have children?" Paige asked.

"They were never blessed with any. He has a niece he's fairly close with." She dabbed at her nose again. "She's going to be crushed." She pulled in a shaky breath. "Thank you for going to check on him. I still can't believe the two of you nearly died as well."

"God certainly was watching over us," Paige said.

Jesse tried not to frown. Was that true? If He was watching, couldn't He have stopped things before they became so intense? Before Rodney died? Before Lydia died, for that matter? *Of course* He could have. And that was why Jesse and God weren't really on speaking terms. Jesse always had a hard time fathoming how horrendous things could happen.

"He certainly was," Bernadette agreed. "I'm so very grateful for that." She seemed to gather some resolve, straightened her spine and said, "I'm glad the two of you stopped by."

Deputy Harris appeared in the hallway. "I'm glad, too," he said. "Bernadette found something." He held up a plastic evidence bag with two small silver objects about the size of quarters. "I took out the batteries."

"What are those?" Paige asked with a frown.

"Surveillance devices," Jesse answered.

"I was determined to find the missing file," Bernadette explained. "I thought maybe it had gotten jammed in a desk drawer. I found one of *those*—" she poked an accusatory finger toward the bag Chad held "—stuck to the side of Rodney's desk instead. I suspected it might be a…a *bug*," she stammered, struggling with the concept. "I thought it best if I checked my own desk and found one there as well."

"I guess that explains how the thugs knew we would be at Mr. Zielinski's house," Jesse said, more to himself than anyone else. "I was wondering about that."

"I didn't find any sign of forced entry," Chad said.

"He probably left the door unlocked while he was

working," Bernadette supplied. "It would be easy for someone to walk in. We grew up in an era when people rarely locked their doors, and security systems were unheard of."

Chad nodded his understanding. "If they did walk right into the building, they likely didn't draw much attention, but I'm going to check with the neighbors. Hopefully, someone saw Mr. Zielinski leave with the perps."

"That would definitely be helpful," Jesse agreed.

"I think I'm done here," Chad said. With a promise to keep Jesse apprised of the situation, he left.

"That young man said he wasn't sure of the cause of death," Bernadette said, her voice quavering. "Do you know anything more?"

"Not at this point, no," Jesse said. He doubted it was carbon monoxide poisoning. It wouldn't have made sense for the thugs to stick around to shut off the car. And clearly, there had been sufficient gas to try to eliminate himself and Paige. "There was no gunshot wound, no visible sign of injury. A toxicology report will be run. We suspect some type of drug overdose." What *he* suspected was that the thugs had drugged the lawyer with chloroform to subdue him and then used something lethal while he was unconscious.

Bernadette looked appalled. "He would *never*—"

"No," Jesse said, placing a comforting hand on her shoulder. "I'm not implying it was his choice."

"Oh. *Oh*," she murmured as understanding took hold. "He truly was murdered."

"We'll know more soon," he said softly.

Bernadette nodded absently, as if she was trying to absorb too much information.

"Is there anything we can do for you?" Paige asked.

Bernadette shook her head. "I'll be all right. I was hoping I could do something for you, though. I searched every nook and cranny for your sister's file."

"Did you find anything?" Paige asked, her tone implying she already knew the answer.

"I'm sorry. I didn't," Bernadette admitted. "I scoured his office, his desk, even his storage closet for good measure. I went over my desk, too, just in case. I just don't understand. Where could it be?" Slowly, realization seemed to take hold. "Whoever planted those devices took it."

Jesse nodded. "Most likely."

"I can't believe someone broke in. They stole from us and bugged us. And if that wasn't bad enough, they abducted poor Rodney and *killed* him." Her voice quivered.

"I'm so sorry," Paige said. "It's a lot to take in."

Bernadette frowned. "Deputy Harris said he doesn't think I'm in any danger, but what do you think?"

Jesse shifted uncomfortably. It was a fair question, but one that was hard to answer. He still didn't have a good enough grasp on this case. "It's hard to say," he admitted. "If you would have asked me yesterday if Mr. Zielinski was at risk, I would've said not likely."

Bernadette stared out the window for a moment, seemingly lost in thought. "My husband and I have been meaning to visit our daughter in Boston," she finally said. "Maybe now would be a good time. Or perhaps we should do something completely unexpected. We could take our RV and go on a long road trip. We've always wanted to visit Canada. There are some beautiful national parks we'd love to see." She wrung her hands, speaking under her breath, clearly agitated and trying to talk through the issue at hand.

"That might be a good option," Jesse encouraged, knowing the farther away from town they got, the better. And if they could leave the country, better still.

"Leo is getting close to retirement," she said. "He has so much vacation time built up that he's about to lose it if he doesn't use it." She sighed. "I had planned on working a few more years, but…" She glanced around the office. "Once I figure out what to do with this place, maybe I'll just retire early. I'd love to have more time to volunteer at the crisis pregnancy center."

"That sounds like a nice idea," Paige said.

Bernadette nodded. "I wish I could be of more help to you," she said. "But there's simply nothing here."

"I appreciate that you took the time to look," Paige said. "It means a lot to me."

Bernadette favored her with a sympathetic smile. "I'll keep scouring my memory, though I can't imagine it'll turn up anything. But if I can do anything to stop whoever killed your sister and my boss, I want to do it." She reached for the laptop case Jesse had seen her set on the floor next to the front door. "If there's nothing else, would you mind walking me to my car? I'll admit I'm feeling a bit skittish. My husband is expecting me home any minute now. After everything that's happened today, I'd hate to keep him waiting. He's already worried enough."

"We'll do better than that," Jesse said. "We'll be happy to follow you home."

"Would you?" The relief and appreciation in her tone were palpable.

"Absolutely," he said. "Any chance you have a se-curity system?"

"We certainly do. And we are vigilant about using it." She paused, and a smile nearly managed to break free. "And we have very nosy neighbors with a very curious dog, so that's even better."

The trio walked outside after Bernadette locked and then double-checked the door. Jesse walked her to her car, and then he and Paige hopped in his truck. As it turned out, Bernadette lived less than five minutes away. That didn't stop him from scouring the street for any sign of malice. When she pulled into her driveway, he pulled over to the curb. She hit the button for the garage door. When it slid up, Jesse couldn't help but cringe, suddenly reminded of being trapped inside the lawyer's garage only hours ago.

"I don't think I'll ever look at garage doors the same again," Paige said quietly. "I think they'll always be a reminder of this ordeal."

He grabbed her hand and squeezed. "At least the or-deal ended well. For us."

"But not for poor Rodney Zielinski," Paige said sadly.

No. Not for Rodney Zielinski. Knowing they had almost shared his fate was too much for Jesse to com-prehend. Anxiety coiled in his stomach. Three attempts on their lives in two days was unacceptable. These men had to be found. In his line of work, he expected to en-counter danger, but the memory of Paige being shot at, fighting with her brakes, then nearly dying in that ga-rage sent determination coursing through him.

He was going to find a way to stop this.

Bernadette had pulled inside her garage, and the door

began to roll down. Knowing she was safely inside, Jesse steered away from the curb.

He felt as if they hadn't accomplished anything today. Well, other than managing to stay alive. But they hadn't found out any information that could help them. However, due to Rodney Zielinski's murder, the Cascade Falls Sheriff's Department was now actively involved.

Sheriff Sanchez was not happy about Paige's attempted murder and Rodney Zielinski's demise happening on her watch. Jesse knew she was digging into the case with astute determination. With the strength of his department behind him, he felt confident they would solve this case. But could they do that before any more lives were lost?

Paige was aware of Jesse's hypervigilance as they drove back to the ranch. The very last thing in the world she wanted to do was bring danger to Molly. She realized he was taking random turns and trekking down unnecessary back roads. The drive took a little longer that way. As anxious as she was to get back to Molly, the extra time was worth their peace of mind. The killers had been in Cascade Falls. And even though they didn't know Paige and Molly's location, the fact they were so close gave her endless chills.

"I'm sorry," she said.

He cast a quick, confused glance her way. "For what?"

"Almost getting you killed." She paused. "Again."

His brow furrowed. "Yeah. Well, that was not your fault. Besides, I face dangerous situations in my job all the time."

"Have you been that close to death before?" Paige asked bluntly.

He hesitated, and she sensed he didn't want to answer.

Finally, he blew out a breath and said, "No."

"He had to have known something," Paige surmised. "Rodney, I mean. Why else would they have gone after him? Why didn't they just steal the file and leave the man alone?"

Jesse's phone rang. He saw that it was Deputy Chad Harris.

"You're on speakerphone, and I'm with Paige," he warned as he answered. "What do you have for me?"

"Not a lot, but it might be something," Chad said. "We got a report on Abe Winslow's financials. Paige mentioned that he was wealthy, but that's not exactly true."

Paige frowned at that surprising revelation, and Jesse darted a questioning glance her way.

"I thought he ran a big-time construction company," Jesse said. Paige nodded her affirmation.

"He does. The company does quite well. That's not the problem." Chad paused and then said, "The guy has a serious gambling problem. He's in debt up to his eyeballs, second mortgage on the house and everything. Looks like he may even have been skimming money from the company, using it for his little problem."

Paige felt her eyes widen in surprise. A gambling problem? Since when? Had Lydia known? Paige was pretty sure Lydia wouldn't have approved of a vice like that. Definitely not if it was severe enough to mortgage the house.

Jesse let out a low whistle.

"Looks like it just started the last few years," Chad added. "But when he got hooked, he got hooked bad."

Jesse thanked him for the information and hung up.

"Do you think that caused stress in the marriage?" he asked.

"She married him because she was tired of living paycheck to paycheck, so yes," Paige said. "That could've caused problems. Maybe she was leaving him because of it, and he was furious about it."

"Maybe," Jesse said. "But marriages fall apart all the time. It doesn't make sense to me that he'd kill her over it. I'm sorry to be blunt," he said gently, "but it's not as if she was killed in the midst of a dispute, in a heated moment. She was on a quiet country road alone with Molly. That suggests planning."

Paige leaned her head against the seat and blew out a breath. "Are you saying you *don't* think she was killed?"

"I'm saying I don't know if Abe is the guilty party here. I don't see a clear motive," Jesse said. "I'm sorry. I know you want—"

"Please don't say I want it to be Abe," Paige grated out. "Because I don't. What I want is answers."

Jesse's phone rang for a second time, and Chad's name once again flashed across the display. Jesse hesitated, as if he didn't want to answer.

"You better get it," Paige said.

"Yeah?" he said by way of greeting.

"Another interesting bit of info just came in," Chad said, sounding intense. "It's about Lydia, but it could definitely relate to her husband. Are you ready for this?"

"Give it to me," Jesse said.

"It appears that Lydia Winslow took out a two-million-dollar life insurance policy." He paused before saying, "On herself."

Paige moaned involuntarily, her hand flying to her mouth. She pressed her fingers over her lips, feeling sick to her stomach. She'd just said she wanted answers, but she wasn't sure she was ready for this.

"Who is the beneficiary?" Jesse demanded.

"That's not listed in the papers I received. We're not sure yet if a claim has been filed. We're looking into it, and the investigation into Lydia's death is being re-opened," Chad said briskly. He explained that Sheriff Sanchez had been in contact with the detective assigned to Lydia's case in Briarville. "They have someone over there questioning Abe Winslow right now. They want to talk to him about Lydia's death and what happened today at Rodney Zielinski's house."

Paige heard Jesse ask Chad a few more questions, but she couldn't concentrate on what they were saying. She'd suspected Lydia was murdered. Was this the missing motive? Was this the proof Jesse and everyone else insisted they needed?

When Jesse disconnected, Paige turned to him.

"Where do we go from here?" Paige asked.

Jesse lifted an eyebrow. "I think you know."

She blew out a defeated sigh. Because yes, she did.

"Tomorrow," Jesse said, "I'm going to pay Abe Winslow a visit."

Paige arched a brow at him. "Not without me, you're not. Lydia was my sister, and this is important to me. I will not be left behind."

He was quiet a moment, as if debating whether or not

to argue. Instead, he simply nodded and said, "Okay. We'll go together."

Together. She liked the sound of that more than she should.

SEVEN

For the second morning in a row, Jesse helped Molly get situated with the little puppy and her bottle. Good old reliable Gus, not wanting to be left out, was curled at their feet. The pup gulped hungrily, making the usual mess along with the adorable slurpy sounds.

"You know," Jesse said, "you and this puppy have a lot in common. You both are surrounded by people who care about you. This little gal was scared when she first came to us."

Molly was too intent on the puppy to look at him, but he was sure she was listening.

"Know what else you have in common?"

She hesitated a moment, as if thinking his question over, then shook her head.

"This little puppy is a fighter. I think you're a fighter, too." He gently rubbed the puppy's ribs, which were filling out nicely. "This little puppy was very afraid when we first got her, but now she knows who she can trust. She can trust us. And so can you." He looked at her expectantly, then realized it was silly to think he could break through when her aunt, whom she already trusted, hadn't been able to.

"Did Erin tell you that I was the one to find this little darling?" he asked.

Molly shook her head.

"I was on patrol," Jesse said. "I saw a box in the ditch. Scared me when the box seemed to tip itself over. Of course, I had to stop to check things out. As soon as I got out of my car, I heard whimpering. I knew there must be some sort of creature in there." There had actually been three little pups only a handful of weeks old in the box. They were all far too young to be away from their mother. The other two had been much weaker and hadn't made it. The memory still made him sad and angry with whoever had dumped them. He certainly wasn't going to share *that* with Molly.

"I brought her to Erin, and she fixed her right up." It hadn't been that simple. He knew Erin had spent a few sleepless nights checking on the little gal and bottle-feeding her every few hours.

Molly's hands were full with the puppy and the bottle, but she still managed to run a thumb sympathetically over the puppy's forehead. The furball closed her eyes, enjoying the touch and the remnants of her milk.

Jesse released an exaggerated sigh. "She's been here almost two weeks, and poor little tyke still doesn't have a name," he reminded her.

Her gaze drifted to him.

"How about… Henrietta?" he suggested.

Molly shook her head.

"Maggie."

She gave him a look.

"What?" he asked with comical huffiness. "It's a popular name. But no? How about Coco Puff? That's cute, isn't it?"

She blew out a sigh.

He snapped his fingers and grinned. "Sassafras!"

She tilted her head to the side, as if seriously contemplating. He thought just maybe they had a winner, but then she cringed apologetically and shook her head.

The puppy finished with the bottle and in a flash squirmed in Molly's lap so she could lick her face. Molly's smile grew as she hugged her firmly.

"Personally, I like the name Briar," Paige said, stepping over Gus so she could join them.

Molly bit her lip.

Jesse chuckled. He got the impression Molly did not agree but didn't want to hurt her aunt's feelings.

Paige scratched the puppy's pudgy belly.

"Guess what, Molly," she said, her tone holding excitement that Jesse knew was manufactured for Molly's sake. "Erin said you were so much help yesterday that she'd love for you to go with her again today. Doesn't that sound fun?" Paige smiled brightly at her niece.

Jesse knew Paige wasn't excited about leaving Molly for a second day. When Erin offered to shuffle her schedule around to take Molly with her again, they couldn't refuse. There was absolutely no way they could bring Molly with them to visit her stepfather. They didn't plan to be gone long, so he hoped it didn't affect Erin's day too intensely.

He had heard back from Chad last night. Chad had given him an update on the Briarville detective's visit with Abe. He'd been at work all day yesterday, his secretary vouching he hadn't left his office. He couldn't possibly be the one who had attacked them in Rodney Zielinski's garage. Not surprisingly, he had denied knowing who Mr. Zielinski was.

True story? Or convenient alibi since he wasn't the kind of guy to get his hands dirty? They still had nothing to tie Abe to Lydia's death or the attacks, so there was nothing that could be done.

Jesse didn't intend to interfere with the investigation, but there were a few questions he wanted to ask the man. He also wanted to see what Abe's reaction to Paige was. If the man wanted her dead, would Jesse be able to tell? Would her presence rattle Abe? Jesse would rather go alone, but Paige had made it clear she wasn't going to be left behind. He wanted to get a feel for Abe. The trip would be worthwhile even if they didn't get any useful information.

"Going with Erin sounds like fun," Jesse supplied.

Molly's smile slipped. While he knew she liked Erin, it was clear she'd rather be with her aunt.

Paige knelt in front of Molly. "I know it doesn't seem fair that I keep running off. I wish I could stay here with you." She reached up and smoothed down Molly's hair. "But Jesse and I have some things to take care of. Adult things that are really no fun at all." She forced a smile. "But as soon as we're able to finish it up, you and I are going to spend a lot of time together. I'm thinking we deserve a movie night with lots of buttery popcorn and root beer floats. Or maybe a game night with pizza. Even better, we could make a weekend of it and do both. Does that sound like fun?"

The child nodded, but it lacked enthusiasm.

Paige's smile slipped away. It was clear she hated disappointing her niece. Jesse understood her need to be with the kiddo right now, her need to bond with her. And as important as that was, making sure she was alive to do it was even more important.

"You know what?" Jesse said. "Erin loves popcorn. She always has some in the cupboard. We won't be gone nearly as long as we were yesterday." He hoped that was true. Barring anyone trying to kill them again, they should be home within a few hours. "How about if we do popcorn and a movie when we get back?"

Before Molly could respond, Erin appeared in the doorway of the utility room.

"Hey there, Molly," she said brightly. "I'm going to check on a newborn foal. I was hoping you'd come with me. How does that sound?"

At the mention of the baby horse, Molly's eyes widened in interest. She slid off the camp chair, kissed the squirmy beagle and handed her to Jesse.

Paige gave her a quick squeeze goodbye, and then Molly left with Erin.

"I hate this," Paige said once they were out of sight. "I hate leaving her behind."

Jesse shifted the wiggly pup from one arm to the other. "You're doing what you need to do."

"That doesn't make it any easier." She pinched the bridge of her nose. "Once this is over, I am going to devote myself completely to being there for her."

He deposited the pooch into the playpen, where she would be safe for the day. The puppy whimpered her protest but then quickly snuggled with her stuffed animal.

He gave Paige's shoulder a squeeze. "Are you sure you're up to this?" he asked. "I could go on my own."

"I need to do this," she said. "I don't know for sure that Abe killed Lydia, but if he did, I want to be able to look him in the face. I want him to know I loved my sister, despite our differences. I wish I had been there for her when she was alive," she said in a wobbly voice. "I'm not going to abandon her now that she's gone. I believe someone killed her. I want that person brought to justice."

Jesse admired her resolve, understood it. He only hoped they didn't get themselves killed trying to follow through.

Paige pulled in a lungful of the cool, crisp spring air. Normally, she'd consider it way too early in the year to drive with the windows down. But Jesse hadn't complained, and she thought perhaps he appreciated the fresh oxygen as well. The ordeal from yesterday was still front and center in her mind, but she needed to push that aside for now. She had a more immediate issue to face.

They were parked outside Hearth & Home Construction. The office was designed to look like a log home, indicative of their specialty. It was located on the edge of Briarville, right off the main road, surrounded by a variety of other businesses. The parking lot held only a few cars, while the pawnshop next door seemed to be bustling. The other businesses within sight had customers coming and going as well. The steady stream of activity—of people—comforted Paige somewhat, because Abe surely wouldn't be so brazen as to try to kill them here in front of his own business, would he? She shuddered at the thought.

"Do you know what he drives?" Jesse asked as he scanned the half-dozen cars in the lot. They had already discussed the fact that Abe may not even be here. He could be out at a job site. If he was, they may just have to linger until he returned, though he knew Paige was anxious to get back to Molly.

"A truck, but I'm not good with makes and models," Paige admitted. "It looked nice, new. All decked out."

Just then, a white full-size pickup truck turned into the lot. The company's logo was decaled on the side. The man wore aviator glasses, but Paige still recognized the profile.

Her eyes widened. "That's him."

Abe cast a cursory glance their way, but he didn't seem too interested as he parked his truck close to the building. If he recognized Paige, who'd ducked her head low, he didn't show it.

"Let's give him a minute to get settled," Jesse said. "I don't want to have this conversation in the parking lot. A customer might stop by, and I'd prefer some privacy."

Paige had told Jesse that Abe had a secretary and a business partner, and the one time she'd visited, it had seemed like he had a busy client schedule. The handful of cars in the lot indicated at least they would not be alone in the small building. If he was guilty, Paige doubted he'd try to pull off anything nefarious with so many potential witnesses. All the same, she knew Jesse was armed, and she felt better for it.

Abe slid from the truck, a stack of papers tucked under his arm. He held his cell phone in the other hand and appeared to be reading messages as he walked. He paid no attention to them at all, but he was likely used to strange vehicles being in the lot as clients showed up for appointments.

Paige scrubbed her hands over her face.

"Are you okay?" Jesse asked softly.

She was touched by the concern in his voice.

Was she okay? She didn't know. Her hands shook, and her stomach rolled, but she had to go through with this. For Molly's sake, and her own, they needed to find out who was behind these attacks. With Lydia gone, all Paige wanted was to create a stable, loving home for her niece. She couldn't do that when bullets were flying.

Maybe she wasn't okay, not really. She was still recovering from yesterday. Still mourning her sister's death. But she could still do this. A Bible verse flitted through her mind.

I can do all things through Christ who strengthens me. It was a simple verse. One of the first she could remember learning, and she knew it was one of the most popular. Probably because it applied so aptly to most things in life. She drew strength from it now. God was with her.

She could do this.

"I'll say a prayer that we get some answers," Paige said, taking a moment to do just that.

"You can pray," Jesse replied lightly when she finished. "I'm going to do some digging."

His response caught her off guard. She arched an eyebrow as she swiveled her head to look at him. "You're not a believer?"

He gave a noncommittal shrug and stared straight ahead at the building. "I wouldn't go that far. It's just that me and God aren't exactly on the same page. Doesn't seem like we ever have been."

"So you do believe," she said slowly. "You're just lacking in faith."

His gaze swung to her. She worried for a moment that she'd offended him, but then he gave a small shrug and simply said, "Something like that."

She sat in silence a moment, letting her mind wrap around his admission. Then she leaned over and clasped his hand, giving it a tight, brisk squeeze. "That's too bad, Jesse. It really is. Because God's there for us. Always. We just need to let Him in."

Afraid he may rebuke her, she busied herself buzzing the window up. Besides, she didn't have time to contemplate his feelings now. They had an important task at hand. "I think we've given Abe enough time to settle in. Let's get this over with."

They strode across the parking lot side by side. Paige wouldn't have been surprised if Jesse could hear the thundering of her heart. It felt as if it may beat right out of her chest. Her hands were cold, clammy. Shaking, she stuffed them in her coat pockets. She realized then that she didn't want Abe to be guilty. She wanted to believe that he and Lydia had grown to love each other, and that in the end, Abe and Lydia had shared a loving marriage. She wanted to think her sister had been happy.

She was afraid that wasn't the case.

Jesse reached the door first and held it open for her. As they had discussed on the drive over, he followed Paige as she breezed past the front desk as if they belonged there.

"Hi, Darci," she said in a no-nonsense tone as she kept right on walking, Jesse only a footstep behind her. She didn't look in the younger woman's direction as she made a beeline for Abe's office. They didn't want to give him a warning of their arrival. She heard Darci sputter something in surprise under her breath, but she didn't leap from her seat and try to block their way.

Paige had stopped at Hearth & Home Construction after the funeral. She and Abe had had a few heated words about the fact that she was taking Molly. The meeting had been tense, but the upside was that she knew exactly where his office was located. She headed straight for it now.

She gave a hard knock on the door frame to announce their arrival and strode in. Jesse closed the door behind them.

"Hello, Abe," she said. "We have a few questions for you."

He glanced up from his computer monitor, a surprised expression on his face. When he realized it was her, his surprise slipped into a scowl.

"You." He pointed an accusatory finger at Paige. "Haven't you caused enough trouble for me? First, you accuse me of killing my wife. And thanks to you, cops showed up at my house, wanting to know if I'm involved in the murder of Rodney Zielinski, a man I've never even heard of."

Paige refused to cower, despite the hatred in his tone.

"You seemed the logical suspect."

"L-logical?" he sputtered. "What did I ever do to you? I barely know you. Your sister didn't want anything to do with you."

Paige winced, because that hurt.

His face reddened. "And as if all that's not enough, you took Molly away from me. Do you realize that I'm the only father she's ever known? I treated her as my own for the past three years!"

"Were you and Lydia having problems?" Jesse asked, his tone a calm contrast to Abe's upset.

Abe moved from behind his desk and strode across the room until he was standing toe to toe with Jesse.

"You look here. Lydia and I may have had an unconventional marriage, but I knew that going in. I was okay with it. I don't care if you believe me or not, but I loved her." He paused, a muscle ticking in his jaw. "Even if she didn't love me."

Paige studied his face. He seemed so adamant. Or was he just a good liar?

Jesse remained calm. "Are you saying that you didn't have any part in her death?"

"In her *accident*?" Abe scoffed. "How could I have?"

"Was she leaving you? Did she ask for a divorce?" Paige asked.

"Of course not!" he cried. "We may have squabbled sometimes, but we always worked everything out."

"Where was she going that night?" Paige asked.

For the first time, Abe's self-righteous facade seemed to crack. An unidentifiable emotion flickered across his face. Was it guilt? Fear? Hurt? She had no idea. She didn't know the man well enough to even begin to try to read him.

"I don't know," he said, his tone low. He pivoted, stepped away from Jesse and returned to the security of his desk. "I don't know," he repeated. "And I don't know why you think I had anything to do with it."

"Molly said so." Paige's words hung in the air for a moment. If she didn't know better, Abe looked stricken. But why? Was he simply afraid of being caught? Or did the words hurt because he was innocent? "When she woke up in the hospital, she said, 'He tried to kill us.'"

"But she never said my name," he growled. "When I was questioned the last time around, my lawyer was sure to clarify that."

"No, she didn't," Paige agreed. "But the moment you walked into the room, her whole demeanor changed.

She went white as her hospital sheet. Didn't you notice the way she shrank away from you? Didn't you notice the look of fear on her face?"

Abe scraped a hand through his hair. His voice was gravelly when he said, "My wife had just died. I didn't notice much of anything."

Paige was torn. She wanted to believe him. She just… didn't. While he claimed he hadn't noticed Molly's fear, she sure had.

"Molly hasn't spoken since that moment. The moment you walked in," she said.

"You think that's my fault!" he shouted. "I love that little girl."

"Do you?" Jesse asked.

Abe's glare was venomous. "Don't you dare question it!" he roared. "I love her like my own. I've been working with my lawyer to determine how to go about getting her back."

Paige's heart dipped into her stomach. "That will never happen!"

"Just watch me," Abe bellowed.

The door flew open unexpectedly. A woman in her forties, platinum blond hair in a perfectly coiffed twist, dressed in beige slacks and a cream sweater, poked her head inside. "Abe," she warned as she nervously fingered the pearls at her neck, "what's the matter with you? Keep it down. We have clients in the waiting room."

He didn't look the least bit chagrined. "Do you know what these two are accusing me of?"

"I don't care. We have a business to run, and you are going to be professional," she scolded. "If you're going to continue this, do it somewhere else." She gave him a

Get up to 4
FREE FABULOUS BOOKS
You Love!

To thank you for being a loyal reader we'd like to send you up to 4 FREE BOOKS, absolutely free.

Just write "YES" on the Loyal Reader Voucher and we'll send you up to 4 Free Books and Free Mystery Gifts, altogether worth over $20, as a way of saying thank you for being a loyal reader.

Try **Love Inspired® Romance Larger-Print** books and fall in love with inspirational romances that take you on an uplifting journey of faith, forgiveness and hope.

Try **Love Inspired® Suspense Larger-Print** books where courage and optimism unite in stories of faith and love in the face of danger.

Or **TRY BOTH!**

We are so glad you love the books as much as we do and can't wait to send you great new books.

So don't miss out, return your Loyal Reader Voucher Today!

Pam Powers

LOYAL READER
FREE BOOKS VOUCHER

YES! I Love Reading, please send me up to 4 FREE BOOKS and Free Mystery Gifts from the series I select.

Just write in "YES" on the dotted line below then return this card today and we'll send your free books & gifts asap!

➡ YES ⬅

Which do you prefer?

☐ **Love Inspired® Romance Larger-Print** 122/322 IDL GRJD	☐ **Love Inspired® Suspense Larger-Print** 107/307 IDL GRJD	☐ **BOTH** 122/322 & 107/307 IDL GRJP

FIRST NAME

LAST NAME

ADDRESS

APT.#

CITY

STATE/PROV.

ZIP/POSTAL CODE

EMAIL ☐ Please check this box if you would like to receive newsletters and promotional emails from Harlequin Enterprises ULC and its affiliates. You can unsubscribe anytime.

LI/SLI-520-LR21

hard look and then turned her gaze to Paige and Jesse. She scowled before tugging the door shut again.

"Who's that?" Jesse asked.

Abe glared at him. "That's none of your business."

"It's Susan Donnelly," Paige supplied. The woman had introduced herself to Paige at the funeral. "She's Abe's business partner."

"She seems friendly," Jesse said snarkily.

There was a knock on the door. Darci, the receptionist, poked her head inside this time. The look she gave them was cold. "Susan took the Tomlins to her office," she said to Abe. "She'll get the meeting started." She winced, as if uncomfortable delivering the rest of the message. "She hopes you'll be along shortly."

"Thank you," Abe said offhandedly.

Darci flashed a smile at him. "You're welcome." Her gaze turned icy as she studied Jesse and Paige. "She asked me to escort *you two* out of the building." Her eyebrow arched, and she straightened her spine. "And if you don't comply, she told me I should call the cops and have them escort you out."

Jesse released a small huff of indignation. Paige couldn't blame him.

"Excellent idea," Abe cried.

Darci's cheeks colored, her lips turning up coquettishly. "It is," she agreed. She held up her phone, clearly enjoying her perceived sense of control. "I can do it right now."

"We're going," Paige said quietly. It wasn't as if they were going to get anything useful out of Abe anyway.

"Don't come back," he childishly shot back at them.

Jesse leveled his gaze at him. "Maybe we will, maybe we won't."

"You had better not," Darci said as she sidled up to her boss.

The way the woman looked at Abe, as if she was desperate for his approval, churned Paige's stomach. Was she just an employee hoping to impress her employer? Or were her feelings deeper than that? What were Abe's feelings on the matter? Right now, he was so worked up, she really couldn't tell.

He huffed out a breath as he glared at her.

Darci scowled and wiggled her phone at them.

Right. They were supposed to be leaving. Jesse started out of the room, and Paige felt there was nothing she could do but follow. As they strode back out to the reception area, past Darci's desk, Jesse glanced out the large window overlooking the parking lot.

"Hey!" he shouted just as Paige caught sight of a man crouching next to Jesse's truck.

What was he doing?

Jesse darted across the room, straight out the front door. He bolted onto the parking lot. Paige was only a few steps behind.

"Call the police!" Paige shouted over her shoulder to Darci, though she had no idea if the young woman would comply.

The guy, wearing a balaclava that was entirely out of place for this time of year, apparently heard the door open. He popped up and took off running. He darted across the slim patch of grass that split Abe's office from the pawnshop.

Jesse took off after him. The man, not the stocky one from the woods, seemed to be in decent shape. He sprinted across the pawnshop parking lot, racing toward the back row of cars. Paige jogged after them, not wanting to lose sight of Jesse. She was trailing them, too far behind to be of any help, when she saw a beige sedan pull out of a spot at the far end of the lot.

Its engine roared, and the man Jesse was chasing darted off to the side.

The next thing Paige knew, the car was charging toward Jesse. She screamed his name and saw him dive. Or was he hit? Had he gone down? She couldn't see him. Didn't know where he'd gone. Didn't know what had happened to him.

Fear tore at her, ripped up and down her spine.

The car screeched to a halt. The man Jesse had been chasing hopped in, and the car tore off. Paige broke into a run. Where was Jesse? Had the man run him over? Her heart felt as if it would beat right out of her chest.

Please, Lord, please, let him be okay.

EIGHT

Jesse had hit the pavement so hard it took him a moment to catch his breath. He'd be the first to admit he wasn't in top condition after yesterday's ordeal. He heard the brakes squeal and half expected the man to back up and try to run him down. He'd managed to roll in between two parked cars so the driver couldn't get to him.

"Jesse!" Paige cried out frantically.

He staggered to his feet. He spotted Paige heading toward him, darting around cars. He didn't miss the look of utter relief when she spotted him. He wanted to go to her, but he scanned the lot for the beige car first. He saw it tearing out onto the main road heading out of town. The car was mud splattered, and the license plate was buried under a layer of grime. He couldn't make out any of it.

Paige jogged up beside him and nearly skidded to a halt as he pulled his new phone out of his pocket. He called 911 to make the report, but by the time he was done explaining the ordeal to the dispatcher, he was sure the pair was long gone. He hung up and slid his phone in his pocket.

When he glanced up, Paige still stood a few feet away. Her arms were wrapped tightly around her waist. Her expression broke his heart. She looked wrecked, the events of the past few weeks continuing to pile on top of her.

As their eyes met, she scooted toward him. "Are you okay?"

When he held his arms out, she slipped into them. He held her close as she gripped his waist tightly, as if she never wanted to release him. Her presence was a calming force. Was it just yesterday that he'd been so determined to keep this woman out of his heart? He was going to have to work harder at that, because if he wasn't careful, she was certainly someone he could fall for. She was brave, determined and *genuine*. Something that Trish clearly had not been.

"I am now," he said. Her hair whispered across his face. He caught the scent of her shampoo. Something citrusy yet sweet.

He wouldn't have minded standing here, holding her for a while longer, letting his adrenaline rush subside while soaking in the presence of this woman he was beginning to care for. Abe strode across the parking lot, Susan and Darci scampering after him. They all wore outraged looks on their faces, as if they were upset at Jesse for nearly getting run over.

Paige slid away from him, though she didn't go far.

"Were those friends of yours?" Jesse asked Abe casually, though his heart was still hammering and his body was thrumming.

"No," Abe said through gritted teeth. "I dare you to find a way to pin this on me."

Darci smirked. "Try it, and his lawyers will eat you alive."

Jesse didn't miss the way Susan winced, or the look of distaste she shot Darci's way. It seemed to him that perhaps she had a great dislike for the company's secretary.

"It's bad enough you took his daughter from him," Darci continued. "It's completely not okay for you to harass him at work." She scowled. "He's going to get Molly back. You just wait and see. And he should. She belongs with him."

"Darci," Abe said, his voice low. "That's enough."

The young woman looked petulant. "It's true."

Jesse felt Paige stiffen beside him. He could almost feel her fear. Only this time, she wasn't afraid for their safety; she was afraid of losing her niece. Jesse had thought Abe was making empty threats in his office, but his secretary had just inadvertently corroborated his story.

"I've had enough of this," Abe said. He took Darci by the elbow and led her back toward the building. The young woman shot a snide look over her shoulder, directing it at Paige, but she didn't protest being dragged away.

Susan shuffled over to them slowly, as if she was afraid they'd blame her for this mess. "Are you all right?" she asked. "Do you need a ride to the clinic? If you want to be checked over, I can drive you."

"I'll be fine. I've been through worse," Jesse assured her.

"Susan," Paige said, her tone imploring, "can you tell me anything about Abe and Lydia's marriage?"

The older woman's eyebrows shot up. "Not really."

But her gaze slid to Abe and Darci, and a distasteful look flashed across her face.

"Not really?" Jesse pressed. "It's my understanding you've been his business partner for quite some time. You must know the man pretty well."

"Correct," Susan said. "I'm his *business partner*. Not his friend. Not his confidante. Our fathers created this business, built it from the ground up. When they retired, I had hoped to buy Abe's father out. Ironically, he'd had a similar hope." She shrugged. "It didn't work out that way. We each inherited half. While I'd rather be in this on my own, we've made it work."

"You don't like having Abe as a partner?" Jesse asked.

"It's fine when his head is in the game. But he's often a little too preoccupied with his…extracurricular activities." She grimaced slightly as she glanced back at Abe and his secretary.

"What activities would those be?" Jesse asked.

Paige raised an eyebrow as Abe and Darci disappeared into the building once more.

Susan waved a dismissive hand at them, ignoring his question. "As long as you're all right, I should get back inside. It's been a busy day. My office overlooks this parking lot. I had my window open a crack to get some fresh air, and when I heard the ruckus, I couldn't help but come outside." She took a step backward. "I really need to get back to work. I believe we've had enough disturbances for one day." She pivoted and hurried away.

Jesse raked a hand through his hair.

"Are you really okay?" Paige asked.

"Yes," he assured her. What were another few bruises

to add to the ones he'd collected yesterday when he'd been knocked out and toppled to a concrete garage floor? Overall, he was fine. "I need to see what that guy was doing to my truck."

He strode toward it, expecting a slashed tire, but it was fine. Had he caught the guy before he did any damage? Or had he been up to something else? He reached under his truck and felt around, tried to visualize where the man's reach had extended.

There.

What was it? He pulled a small black device from the backside of his rear fender.

"I'm guessing that's too small to be a bomb," Paige said flatly. Still, she glared at the object with disdain.

"It's a tracking device," Jesse confirmed. He glanced around the parking lot and then walked toward the garbage can outside the building. On the way, he discreetly wedged the device into the crease of Abe's bumper. He threw away a stray gum wrapper from his pocket and then strode back to Paige as if that had been his sole intent.

"We'd better get out of here." Paige glanced over her shoulder nervously.

"I was thinking the same thing," he agreed. "I wouldn't be surprised if they switch out their vehicle and loop back around."

They hustled to his truck, got in, and Jesse left the lot, going the opposite direction the men had. He took a few random turns while keeping a close watch in his rearview mirror. It was early afternoon, and most people still seemed to be at work, so traffic was light.

"I haven't noticed anyone," Paige said. "Have you?"

He realized she had her eyes glued to the passenger mirror.

"I think we're in the clear," he agreed.

"What do you think Susan meant by 'extracurricular activities'?" Paige wondered. "Do you think she was talking about Darci? Do you think he could've been having an affair? Maybe even still is?"

"Anything is possible," Jesse said.

"I don't know where to go from here," Paige admitted. "I don't know why I'm so disappointed in our conversation with Abe. It's not like I believed he'd confess to killing Lydia or Rodney." She paused. "But I thought he'd give us *something*."

"That's the way investigations go," Jesse said. "Sometimes it can be a whole lot of legwork and not a lot of payout. The hope is always that something will eventually shake loose. If Abe's guilty, I don't think it hurts to let him know he's on our radar. It just might make him back off."

Or he might come at them full force to try to get them out of the way. No sense mentioning that. It was obvious Paige already had enough to worry about.

"Do you think he can take Molly from me?" she asked, her voice quaking.

"He never formally adopted her, did he?"

"No," Paige said. "But he has money. And a lawyer. And Molly did live with him for half her life."

"Actually, he doesn't have money," Jesse reminded her. "Come to think of it, maybe his gambling problem is the 'extracurricular activity' Susan was referring to. She seems like she's very involved in the business. If he's skimming money off the top, she's probably aware of it."

"Right," Paige said. "I can't believe I forgot about that. I've always thought of him as wealthy. It's hard to wrap my head around the fact that he's not."

"I don't think you have anything to worry about. He has no legal claim to Molly. Lydia was her mother, and she took precautions to be sure that *you* have her daughter. Not Abe," Jesse assured her. "He may have a lawyer, but I don't think he has a legal leg to stand on."

"That's what I thought, too," Paige said. "But he seemed so—"

"Arrogant about it?" Jesse said. "He seems like a man used to getting what he wants. But this time, the law isn't on his side. There won't be anything he can do."

Paige nodded, but Jesse didn't think she was going to relax anytime soon.

Since the moment Abe had threatened her, a new sense of fear had snaked around Paige's heart, gripping her hard. She had already lost her sister. She couldn't lose Molly, too. Lydia had entrusted her child to her, and she would do anything within her power for that little girl.

"You're still upset about Abe's threat, aren't you?" Jesse asked quietly.

Was he already able to read her so well? Or was she just that obvious?

They were halfway back to the ranch. Paige had checked in with Erin. She would bring Molly back to the ranch, grab a quick lunch and head back to work. Paige could hardly wait to see her niece. She'd loved her from the moment she was born. She had sent gifts, letters and cards even during the time she and Lydia weren't speaking. These past few weeks, everything had shifted. She felt responsible for her, attached to her in a way that she never had before.

"I don't want to let him get to me," Paige said, "but I can't help it. I wonder if he really wants Molly, or if he just doesn't want me to have her."

"That's hard to say," Jesse admitted. "If I had to guess, I'd say he's attached to her. He was pretty emotional when he was talking about her in his office."

Paige frowned. "The man in the woods," she started to say. "Remember when he said that they were after me, but that Molly shouldn't be hurt?"

"Yes," Jesse said, "I've been thinking about that, too."

"Maybe that's Abe's motive," she reasoned. "Maybe he wants me out of the way, because without me, he thinks he can get Molly back."

"The thought crossed my mind," Jesse admitted. "Maybe he had Lydia killed for her life insurance policy. He probably never thought she'd appoint you guardian in her will."

"He thought Lydia was expendable, but he cares for Molly?" Paige asked.

A few beats of silence filled the truck as they thought that over.

"It doesn't quite sit right, does it?" Jesse asked. "I feel like we're still missing something. It's hard to believe he'd kill Lydia and then expect to raise Molly as his own with that secret lingering over them."

"Unless he doesn't really love Molly like he claims," Paige said. "Maybe he just doesn't like the thought of losing. Like she's his possession. Something he's not willing to give up."

"I guess there's always that possibility," Jesse said.

"I hate the thought of her going back to him." Paige shuddered. "If I'm out of the picture, what's that going to mean for Molly?"

"You've never mentioned your parents. Would they take her? Not that I think anything is going to happen to you," he quickly clarified. "I'm just wondering where they stand."

Paige shook her head. "Our dad took off when Lydia and I were small. I barely remember him. Mom was young when she had us. She hated being a single parent. She never said it, but I know she was relieved when Lydia and I left home and she didn't have to be responsible for us anymore. I can't imagine her wanting to take in a six-year-old at this point in her life."

"Nothing is going to happen to you," Jesse said firmly, "so don't waste time worrying about that."

Paige knew worry accomplished nothing. Furthermore, she knew the Bible warned against it. Yet, try as she might, she couldn't help it. Molly's future was at stake. What if Abe managed to kill her? What if Abe went to prison? Where would Molly go? Would her precious niece end up in the system?

"Were foster homes awful?" Paige asked almost without meaning to, but that was where her thoughts had drifted.

Jesse glanced over at her and shrugged. "I really can't say. I wasn't in any of them long enough to find out. I had a habit of running away days after I was placed," he admitted. "Foster parents didn't like that type of liability, losing a kid on their watch, so it got harder to find somewhere to send me."

"How did you go from being a foster kid to a deputy?" she wondered. "If you don't mind me asking."

She realized it might be a terribly personal question, but she was curious. Also, she really wanted to think about something other than her own ordeal, at least for a little while.

"To answer that," Jesse said, "I'll have to go way back. The spring I turned thirteen, I came home from school one day, and my mom was gone. At first, I didn't think much of it. She wasn't a great mom," he said quietly. "I was left alone a lot. After several days, I started to worry. I noticed she'd cleaned out her closet, her dresser. I started to realize she probably wasn't coming back. It took a couple weeks before the electricity went out. Obviously, she'd stopped paying the bill at some point. Around that time, I'd finished off every bite of food in the house. I was starving."

The admission made Paige's heart twist in sympathy. Her mom hadn't been the most attentive, but at least all of her basic needs had been met. She'd never been abandoned.

"We lived in a trailer park on the edge of town." He glanced at her, his expression shadowed. "I walked to a gas station, stole a box of crackers and a jar of peanut butter. It wasn't the first time I'd stolen food, I'm not proud to say. That time, a deputy met me on the sidewalk as I walked out of the building. The owner had recognized me, knew what I was up to, and had called the cops when he saw me approaching."

Paige winced.

He smiled. "It turned out to be a blessing in disguise. Hank Cooper was on duty that day."

"Hank Cooper?" Paige echoed. "Erin's dad?"

"One and the same." Jesse went on to tell Paige how Hank had brought him back to the trailer, intent on talking to his parents. It had taken a matter of minutes for Hank to realize that Jesse had been abandoned. After realizing why Jesse was stealing food, he'd taken him out to eat. He'd taken the time to really listen to what Jesse had to say, which at that time hadn't been much. Jesse had insisted he was fine on his own. He was used to it, and he didn't need anyone. Eventually, Deputy Cooper had to call Child Protective Services.

"I thought I'd never see the guy again," Jesse admitted. "But he was the one to find me and drag me back a few of the times I ran. One day, my social worker told me she was out of options. I'd have to go to a group home." His lips quirked. "I'll never forget Hank striding in, wearing this determined look." Jesse explained that Hank had asked to speak with the social worker in the hallway. They were out there for a while, and when they came back, Hank announced he and his wife had become licensed foster parents and were going to bring Jesse home. "I was young and naive at the time. I had no idea that they'd become licensed specifically to take me in." He gave her a sheepish grin. "Somehow, during all the times he picked me up, I apparently grew on Hank. I learned later that it hadn't taken much to convince Ellen they should take a chance on me.

"I ran away from Hank and Ellen a few times, too. Finally, Hank sat me down. He reminded me that winter was coming. It was going to get cold. The abandoned buildings I'd been frequenting were going to be miserable. Quite bluntly, he told me I'd be a fool not to stay put in a warm, cozy house where I knew I'd always be safe, warm and fed." He let out a self-deprecating laugh. "At first, I was furious that he called me out like that, but then the snow started to fall, and I realized, in all my thirteen-year-old wisdom, that he was right. So I stayed put. And I realized that living with the Coopers wasn't so bad. Back then, I didn't see much of Erin. By the time I settled down, she was off at school. She came home on weekends but spent a lot of time with friends. I didn't think she was too bad, so I didn't mind having her around. It wasn't until she finished school and moved back to Cascade Falls that we started to get close." He smirked. "She'll be the first to tell you she prayed for years for a baby sister, but Ellen couldn't have more kids. She says God answered her prayers by giving her a wild, defiant teenage brother."

Paige smiled at that. "The Coopers never adopted you?"

"It wasn't for lack of their asking," he assured her. "Even though I settled in, I was still a pretty rebellious teen. It wasn't until I was in my early twenties that I *really* understood what they had done for me. Even after I turned eighteen, technically aging out of the system, they kept me around, insisting I show up for family dinners and holidays and everything in between. They helped me get on my feet. Hank helped me get a job with a landscaping company. I liked it, but it wasn't a career. A few years into it, I knew I wanted more out of my life. It hit me that I wanted to be like Hank, the only dad I'd ever known. They paid my way through the police academy, cheered me on, showed up for my graduation. Hank helped me get a job with the department. We worked together for just under two years before he retired."

Paige's heart warmed at the thought of this couple she'd never met. Her admiration for them soared. She found herself thinking how lovely it would be to meet them someday.

"Eventually, I came to my senses and realized they are my family, but it took me a good decade to do so," he admitted. "But no, they never officially adopted me. I don't need a piece of paper from the courts to tell me that."

"And your mom?" Paige asked. "Your birth mom, I mean." Because he clearly considered Ellen to be his mother, as well he should.

"When I was younger, I was convinced something tragic had happened to her. I just knew she had to be dead. Why else wouldn't she come back for me?" Jesse asked. "But Hank told me he'd been keeping track of her. Last I checked, she was waitressing over in Aspen. I didn't look into her any more than that. She left me and never looked back. I'm not happy about it, but I think I've made peace with it." He looked contemplative. "I think everything worked out the way it was supposed to. I wouldn't have the job I have, wouldn't be living the life I'm living, if she'd stuck around. I'm sure about that."

"It sounds like you found the most wonderful family," Paige said, her voice wistful as they turned into the ranch where Erin and Molly were waiting.

Gus trotted off the porch to greet them, tail wagging.

"I sure did," Jesse said. "I honestly don't know where I'd be today without them."

Would she ever be able to provide a support system like that for Molly? Would they ever have such loving people in their lives? Would Paige be enough for her?

And the biggest question of all, would she even be alive to see her niece grow up?

NINE

Paige sat on the bottom porch step. Jesse sat next to her. He wasn't close enough that they were touching, but she could smell the crisp, clean scent of the soap he used. She could even feel some of the warmth radiating off his body. She wanted to lean into him, but she refrained, uncomfortable with how much she had come to depend on him in such a short amount of time. God willing, this would all be over soon. She would go back to Grand Junction. Jesse would stay here in Cascade Falls, where his home, his family and his job were.

Two days had gone by since Jesse had nearly been run down in the parking lot. There were no new leads. She felt no closer to catching her sister's killer. Jesse had warned her these things took time, but the waiting was *so* hard. Patience had never been a virtue she possessed, and spending time with Jesse was becoming treacherous to her heart.

As much as she longed for the day that this would be over so she could concentrate on being a parent to Molly, she dreaded Jesse walking out of her life. It was silly, really. There were a few brief moments where she thought perhaps there'd been a spark of something between them, but there were also many moments where Jesse remained reserved. She needed to remind herself that he was helping her because that was what he did.

It was his job.

His life's calling.

She pushed aside her thoughts about Jesse. None of that really mattered. Not only did he not seem interested in her in a romantic way, but she shouldn't be interested in him either. She needed to be able to direct her full attention to Molly. Raising her niece needed to be her top priority. It seemed selfish, in a way, to even entertain the idea of a romantic endeavor with so much going on.

They chuckled as they watched Molly play with the puppy on the lawn. Erin had found a small tug rope. The puppy had one end, Molly the other. Molly would tug, but the moment the beagle seemed ready to release, Molly relented, as if she felt bad about taking the pup's toy away. As they played, Gus darted around them in gleeful circles. The German shepherd looked enormous compared to the little beagle.

"It's good to see her so happy," Paige said. They had just finished dinner dishes, and Erin was in the barn, checking in on the pregnant cat a client had found hiding in their woodpile. The horses were frolicking in the pasture, and Paige thought this was exactly what a rescue ranch should be.

"She does love that puppy," Jesse surmised. "You might need to bring it home with you."

"I think I need to concentrate on taking care of Molly," Paige said. "I don't know if I have the energy to bring a puppy into the mix." She sliced a sly glance his way. "Why don't you keep her?"

Jesse looked contemplative. "I just might. Erin's always trying to get me to take one of the strays she ends up with." He smiled at the pup. "I do feel pretty attached to this one."

He had told Paige how he'd found the poor thing in the ditch.

Without warning, the puppy let go of the tug rope and took off after Gus. Molly dropped the rope and followed. In seconds, the two dogs and the child were engaged in what looked like a mishmash game of tag.

Paige's heart swelled with love for Molly. It felt good to sit here relishing the moment. She knew the police were trying to find a connection between Abe and her attackers. Jesse had mentioned that they'd obtained video footage from outside Mr. Zielinski's law firm as well as outside of the Hearth & Home Construction office yesterday. She prayed the thugs had slipped up and revealed themselves, but so far, she and Jesse hadn't heard anything about their identities.

The toxicology report had confirmed Jesse's suspicion. Rodney Zielinski had died of a heroin overdose. The working theory was that he'd been chloroformed after he was kidnapped and then injected with a lethal dose of heroin. It was a small consolation, but Paige was relieved he'd likely been unconscious for much of his ordeal.

When her phone rang, she jumped. She'd forgotten she'd slid it into her pocket. It had been days since she'd received a call. She glanced at the screen, then at Jesse. Her heart gave a hard thud. "I don't recognize the number."

When she answered, she was prepared to hear a threatening voice. Instead, she was greeted softly by a voice that she thought she recognized but couldn't quite place.

"Yes, this is Paige," she replied.

"Hello, there. This is Bernadette from Rodney Zielinski's.office."

"Hi, Bernadette," Paige said, her gaze locked with Jesse's, and his eyebrows hitched. "How are you?" She knew that Deputy Harris had spoken with her recently and updated her on her employer's cause of death.

She leaned toward Jesse, tilting the phone so he could hear as well.

"I'm doing all right," she said. "I know I talked about leaving town, but I just couldn't until I wrapped up a few things for the office. It's probably silly, I know, since I don't know what's going to happen to the practice now that Rodney is gone." Her voice shook, and she took a moment to compose herself. "I'm sure you're wondering why I'm calling, so I'll get right to it. I was going through billing statements, and it occurred to me there should be one for your sister."

"Oh." The small sound of surprise escaped from Paige's lips. "Did you find one?"

"I did," Bernadette said. "I don't know how helpful it will be. But at least it proves she was a client. I enter all of our invoices electronically, then print them off and send them out in weekly batches. I have a copy of hers, if you'd like me to send it to you."

"Yes, I would most definitely like that," Paige said.

"We should go pick it up," Jesse whispered.

Paige nodded. "Actually, would it be all right if we stopped by to get it?"

The woman hesitated a moment. "I suppose that would be all right. If you can get here within the hour.

My husband and I are packed and ready to go. He's just puttering around with some last-minute things on the motor home."

"We'll be there," Paige said. "See you soon."

"Goodbye, dear."

The line disconnected.

"If she's going out of town," Jesse said, "this could be our last chance to touch base with her for a while. I think it would be good to see her in person. Now that she found that billing statement, maybe it'll rattle her memory free. She was pretty distraught when we first met her, when Rodney didn't show up for work, and even more distraught after. She was definitely not thinking clearly then."

Paige nodded her agreement and then winced. "Molly."

"I'll talk to Erin," Jesse said. "I'm sure she won't mind."

"Your sister is so sweet. She wouldn't admit it if she did mind." She wrapped her arms around her middle, looking defeated. "I feel bad, though. I feel bad I'm not spending more time with Molly, and I feel bad that I'm relying on your sister so much."

"It's okay," Jesse said. "Or it will be. That's why we're doing this. We need to get to the bottom of things. And while I have full faith in my department, it doesn't hurt to look into all avenues."

"I can't imagine a billing statement will have much information," Paige said, "but we don't have anything else to go on right now."

"I'll talk to Erin," Jesse said. "You can let Molly know. Then we better head out so we don't hold Bernadette up."

* * *

Half an hour later, they pulled up to the curb at Bernadette's house. An older man with graying hair and a sturdy physique nodded to them as he balanced a box in one arm and tugged open the door of the RV. Bernadette stepped onto the porch and waved at them.

Not wanting to hold the couple back any longer than they had to, Jesse and Paige rushed up the sidewalk.

"Thanks for waiting for us," Paige said.

"Your timing is perfect," Bernadette replied. "Leo couldn't get his request for time off approved until some crucial paperwork was done, but he just got off work a bit ago. We're going to head out tonight, just in time for the weekend. We have a reservation at a campground several hours from here. It'll be dark when we get there, but quite frankly, I'm so anxious to get out of town that I don't really care." She stepped back. "Come on inside."

Jesse ushered Paige in. Though he didn't think they'd been followed, he wouldn't put it past the murderer to be keeping an eye on Bernadette's house. One last, quick scan of the street didn't entirely appease him. A jogger was headed their way. A mother pushed a stroller while a child rode on his bike. In the other direction, he spotted a skateboarder. There were too many cars parked on the street of this busy neighborhood, as far as he was concerned. A few had tinted windows, which he didn't like at all.

He felt a bit of relief when the door closed behind them. At least no one would take a shot at them while they lingered outside for too long. He was grateful that Leo was now puttering around the motor home, checking all the tires. Hopefully, the man's presence in the yard would keep any thugs away.

Bernadette plucked a manila envelope off a decorative table in the entryway. She handed it to Paige.

Before Jesse could question her, she surprised him by saying, "I remembered something."

"About Lydia?" Paige asked, her voice full of hope. She clutched the envelope, containing the billing statement, to her chest.

Bernadette nodded. "Yes. I didn't recognize her immediately. She was in a while ago, and Rodney did have a fair number of clients. However, I couldn't stop looking at her picture the other night. There was something niggling at me—I just couldn't remember what it was. When I scanned over her billing statement, it came to me."

Both Paige and Jesse looked at her expectantly.

"There was a notary fee on her bill," Bernadette said. "We don't charge much, only two dollars. Anyhow, that got me to thinking. I remembered I notarized something for her. I just couldn't remember *what*."

"But you did remember?" Paige asked hopefully.

"Oh, yes," Bernadette said, "I did. It's not my job to look over what I'm notarizing. My job is to simply determine that the correct person is signing the paper. However, I do have to scan the page just a bit to see where the signatures go, the notary stamp, the date and whatnot." She paused, a frown carving deep creases between her eyebrows. "Your sister had me notarize a life insurance policy."

"You're sure about that?" Jesse asked.

"Very sure," Bernadette said. "It wasn't just the policy, though. It was a change-of-beneficiary form for a policy that was already in place." Her furrow deepened.

"Is that something that's typically notarized?" Paige asked.

Good question, Jesse thought.

"No, it's not," Bernadette said. "I think that's why it sticks out in my mind. Once I remembered your sister, the memories started rolling back to me. There's not even an official place on the form for a notary to sign. I think that's why I did such a thorough perusal of it before I realized. When I told her we don't usually need to notarize change of beneficiaries, she told me it didn't matter. She wanted it notarized regardless."

"She knew something was wrong," Paige said quietly.

Jesse said nothing, but he had to agree.

"Looking back, I think she did," Bernadette said. "I clearly recall her saying she wanted it notarized because she didn't want to leave any room for doubt."

The words raked down Jesse's spine.

"Do you recall who the beneficiaries were?" he asked. "The old and the new?"

"I don't."

Jesse and Paige shared a troubled glance.

"I don't suppose you have a copy of it?" he asked, though he was sure of the answer.

She shook her head. "No. It's not something we typically keep. Although, given the circumstances, Lydia may have asked Rodney to keep a copy. I doubt he did, because he didn't ask me to make a copy, and it wasn't often he used our persnickety copier on his own if he didn't have to." She sighed. "And as you know, if it was in her file, it would be gone regardless."

The door creaked open, and Leo stepped in. "Don't

mind me. I have one more load to take out." He side-stepped them and bounded up the stairs.

"This information has been very helpful," Jesse said. "Is there anything else that you remember?"

"There's not," Bernadette said. "However, if I do remember, I have your numbers."

"We should go, then," Paige said. "We've already kept you long enough. I can't tell you just how sincerely we appreciate your time."

Bernadette gave her a tremulous smile. "I'm happy to help. I am not really a believer in coincidences. I think whoever killed your sister killed Rodney, too. I worked for him for a lot of years. He was a good boss. A good man. If I can help in any way to bring his killer to justice, I'll do it."

"I hope you and your husband are able to enjoy your vacation," Jesse said. "Be safe."

"You as well," Bernadette said.

Jesse hustled Paige down the sidewalk. Though no one in particular had him on edge, he'd be happy when they were away from here. The trip had been worth it, because as he'd anticipated, Bernadette had come up with more information while she waited for them to arrive. He hoped she and Leo would get out of town safely. They should, since they were no real threat, and it would take extra resources to trail someone out of town.

He drove to a gas station a few blocks away. He didn't need to fill up, but he wanted to get a view of the cars going by to be sure they weren't being followed. He chose a quiet gas station on the edge of town and pulled into a spot on the side of the lot.

Paige had been silent until now. When she spoke, she sounded so bereft it nearly broke his heart. "She really was afraid for her life," Paige said. "She had to be. Everything points to it. She created her will and changed her life insurance beneficiary." She pulled in a shaky breath. "I wish she would've come to me. I wish she would've known that I'd do anything to help protect her."

"Hey," Jesse said and took her hand. "I'm sure she knew you loved her. Think about it, Paige. If she really thought her life was in danger, maybe that's why she *didn't* go to you. Maybe she didn't want to put you at risk, too."

She shrugged. "I guess I'll never know."

No. She never would.

"It's not strange that she had a life insurance policy on herself," Paige surmised. "I have a policy through my job."

"I do, too," Jesse said, "but the amount of Lydia's policy seems excessive."

Paige blew out a sigh. "I've been trying to rationalize it. I told you that after Tom died, she was bereft. She was in dire straits financially, so maybe she wanted to be sure that never happened again. I'm sure she wanted Molly cared for if something happened to her. And since Molly is so young, it wouldn't make sense to make *her* the beneficiary. Lydia would know that I'd only use what I needed to care for Molly and give her the remainder of it when she becomes an adult."

"You think the policy was Lydia's idea?" Jesse asked.

"I don't know, but I don't think it would've taken much to convince her to take it out," she admitted. "Having lost Tom, death and its aftermath were very real to her."

"Maybe you should open that," Jesse said, indicating

the envelope. He scanned the road, the parking lot, the venues across the street. As far as he could tell, they weren't being tailed.

Paige didn't need prodding. The envelope wasn't sealed, so she simply untucked the flap. She pulled out the single sheet of paper. Of course, the logo of Rodney's office was on top. She scanned the bill, line by line, with Jesse peering over her shoulder. There were office hour fees, phone fees, the notary fee.

"I haven't seen a lot of billing statements from lawyers' offices," he admitted, "but it all looks pretty standard to me."

"Me too," Paige said. "It looks like she met with him twice. It doesn't specify what the visits were for, just that there were office visits. I suppose the first time to go over everything, the second to sign the finalized copies, and a handful of phone calls in between. I wonder who called who," she mused. "I suppose it doesn't matter. I assume it was to iron out details." She began to slide the statement back into the envelope, but with a sharp gasp, she pulled it back out.

Jesse was instantly alert. Paige pointed to the address on the page. It was placed so that when the paper was folded, the address would be visible through the window of an envelope. She glanced at him, confusion etched into her features. "That's not Paige's address."

He cocked an eyebrow at her. "Are you sure?"

"Yes." She paused. "I mean, it's not her house in Briarville where she lived with Abe. It's a Grand Junction address," she murmured. "Could she have moved out? Wouldn't that have raised flags during the police investigation?"

"You'd think it would be worth noting," Jesse said. "And Abe never mentioned it."

"We asked him where he thought she was going that night. He said he didn't know."

Jesse pulled out his phone, punched in some information, and moments later, a GPS map loaded. "This is the address. It's about an hour from here."

She took the phone, studied the route and placed her hand over her mouth. Jesse noticed the color drain from her face.

"What's wrong?"

"Jesse, this road." She enlarged the screen and pointed to a squiggly line. "This one right here? Balsam Ridge Road? This is where she died."

Their eyes met as they simultaneously came to the same conclusion.

"She left him that night," Jesse said. "And she was on her way to her new house."

Paige nodded. "I think so."

Jesse glanced at the screen again. "Did you notice this? The property is on a lake. There're two structures at this address. I wonder if she rented a lake cottage from the owner of the property. That's what it looks like to me. If that's right, there's a chance the owner of the property will be around."

Paige nodded, understanding where his train of thought was headed. They just might make contact with one more person they could question. One more person who'd spoken with Lydia during her last days.

"It's getting late, and Molly will be going to bed soon. How do you feel about checking this place out? I think we can make it there around dark, maybe a bit before," he said.

"I'd like to go," Paige agreed. "If you're sure Erin won't mind."

"I know she won't," he assured her. He took his phone back from Paige and sent his sister a text to give her an update. She was quick to reply that they should do whatever they needed to do. She and Molly had built a blanket fort in the living room. They were currently inside of it playing Connect 4 and would be just fine.

"That settles that," Jesse said. With one final perusal of the area, they rolled out of the parking lot. "Let's see if we can find where your sister was going to live."

Half an hour later, Jesse was second-guessing their decision. The road was winding, so travel was slower than he'd anticipated, and it would be dark by the time they reached their destination. He wasn't sure what they'd be able to glean in the dark, and they'd still have to travel back to the ranch.

"Are you doing okay?" Jesse asked. He knew it had to be hard for Paige to be riding on the same road where her sister was killed. Due to taking care of Molly, she had not seen the place where her sister went off the edge. Now that he was driving it, in the dark no less, he could see how easy it was to go off the road. The embankment was steep in most places, and the curves in the road seemed never-ending.

"I'm fine," Paige said. "It just feels surreal. Since I haven't been out this way, I don't know where she died. I don't know if we've passed it already or if it's coming up," she said, her tone strangled.

"I shouldn't have suggested we do this tonight," Jesse said. "It was impulsive. I didn't think it through."

"Neither did I," she said. "But I feel like it's something we need to do, so maybe it's best to just get it over with."

True, he thought. But making the trek in daylight might've been a wiser option. The sun had set now, and darkness blanketed the sky.

"Do you think Bernadette should make an official statement to the police?" Paige asked. "Would it help if she let them know Lydia changed the beneficiary?"

"What would help," Jesse said, "is to know who the two people listed are. We need to find out who the current beneficiary is."

"How could someone kill another human being for *money*?" she choked out.

"I don't know," he said honestly. "But it definitely wouldn't be the first time. And with Abe's financial problems…" He let the rest of that thought just hang in the air. In part, because clarification wasn't needed. But also because a car had been following them for several miles now. That in itself wasn't too strange. There weren't a lot of places to turn off on this road. What did bother him was that the car had kept a nice wide distance between them. But not now. Now it seemed to be gaining on them.

And quickly.

"I hate to say it," Jesse muttered under his breath, "but I think we might have company."

"What?" Paige whirled around, looking over her shoulder out the back window. "Where did that car come from? I've been watching the side mirror."

"It's been following for a while, but so far back it wasn't visible around the curves," he said. "Like now."

She nodded as the car disappeared again. "I see what you mean."

The car reappeared, even closer than before.

"Suddenly, they've sped up and are gaining on us. Fast." He gripped the steering wheel of the truck. There was nowhere to pull over. The shoulder was minimal. To his right, the hillside dropped off substantially. To his left, the hillside towered above them. They hadn't met many cars going the opposite direction, but with so many curves, he needed to be sure to stay out of the lane of oncoming traffic. If someone was headed toward them, it would be too late by the time they were visible rounding a curve.

With that thought, the vehicle trailing them burst around the curve they'd just rounded. The headlight beams were on bright, reflecting in the rearview mirror, momentarily blinding Jesse. Starbursts of light exploded behind his eyelids, stealing his vision. He let out a growl of frustration, knowing the road curved any second, just unsure of when.

For a fraction of a second, fear slammed into him. They couldn't go over the edge. Not here. Not when the incline was so steep. He didn't want them to end up like Lydia.

Please, God! The prayer wasn't much, but it was all he had time for.

"Jesse!" Paige screamed.

He yanked the steering wheel to the left. His truck careened across the road into the oncoming traffic lane. They slammed to a halt as his front bumper crashed into the steep incline. He blinked away the stars flashing behind his eyes. He was only vaguely aware of a vehicle, the same beige sedan they'd seen before, swerving around them. The sedan's engine screamed as it flew past.

Jesse gripped the steering wheel, breathing hard. His hands were slick on the steering wheel as his heart beat frantically. He only took a moment to get his wits about him. Then he slammed the truck into Reverse. He quickly maneuvered back into his own lane in case there was any oncoming traffic headed their way.

"What happened?" Paige asked. "Why did you go off the road like that? Were you afraid they were going to rear-end us?"

Ignoring her question, he asked, "Are you all right?" They'd hit the incline hard.

"I'm... Yes, I'm fine," she decided. "You?"

"I am," he said, blinking hard again, his vision finally clearing some. He'd like to pull over, take a minute to gather himself, but with no shoulder, that wasn't wise. He could see the centerline, so he followed that, only going a fraction of the speed limit. "But there's something you should know."

"What?" she asked, sounding completely perplexed.

"When they came up behind me out of nowhere, they flicked their high beams on," he said.

"Yes," Paige agreed, nodding emphatically. "They lit up the car."

"For just a few moments, when it reflected off the mirror, I was blinded. I couldn't see where the road was. I didn't want to go over the edge."

"Oh, Jesse," she said, her tone full of compassion, "that's why you drove us into the other lane. It was safer over there."

"Right," he agreed. He glanced at her, his vision almost entirely returned by now. The dashboard lights illuminated her pretty, concerned face. "That's not all, Paige."

"What do you mean?"

"I think they may have done the same thing to your sister," he said, his tone quiet. "The police report couldn't find a reason for the accident. There was no indication of her being run off."

"But if someone came up and blinded her, and she couldn't see…" She choked back a sob. "She told Molly someone was trying to kill them. She knew someone was coming up behind her. She would've had nowhere to go."

And they had nearly met the same fate.

TEN

Jesse drove several more miles before he finally found a side road to turn onto.

"Why are we stopping?" Paige asked. She glanced around, taking in the desolate surroundings. They were finally on flatter terrain. Deep woods lined both sides of the road. The GPS hadn't told them this was where they needed to turn.

Jesse parked the truck, reached across her and pulled his Maglite out of the glove box. "Something has been bothering me. How did they know where we were? I waited at the gas station, watching traffic. I kept an eye out and didn't notice anyone until after we turned off. So how did they know we'd be on Balsam Ridge Road?"

It was a rhetorical question, and he slid from the truck before Paige could answer. She hopped out and found him crouched down, running his hand along the underside of the truck as he'd done at Abe's office the other day. He crab-walked forward, feeling the undercarriage.

She glanced around. The darkness seemed almost overwhelming. Night had fallen fast and now blanketed them. It was easy to imagine someone stalking them through the trees, though she really didn't think that was the case. But still, she was glad she wasn't alone. Yet again, she was hit with a wave of gratitude that Jesse was with her. On the side of the road, at night, in the middle of nowhere was just about the last place she wanted to be.

Finally, his face turned to stone. "You have *got* to be kidding me," he growled. He plucked another small tracking device from under his truck.

Paige gasped, more in indignation than surprise. "Where did that come from?"

He stood and stomped on it until it shattered. "I don't know. There were so many people on Bernadette's street. I remember seeing a jogger. All he'd have to do is stop, pretend to tie his shoe and slide it right on. I don't know if it was him. Could've been someone else. I just didn't think they'd try the same trick twice." He frowned. "Leo was outside most of the time, but he came in at the end of our visit. It wouldn't have taken someone long at all to plant it."

Paige could tell he was giving himself a mental lashing over this. She couldn't stand for that. "Don't beat yourself up over this. These people have been relentless. You can't be in two places at once," she said soothingly. "You couldn't have stayed outside to keep watch *and* come in to help me question Bernadette. We've been running nonstop. You've saved my life multiple times. I think it's safe to say you've had a lot on your mind. Besides—" she reached up, gave his shoulder a squeeze "—what's important is that you figured it out now, before we got to Lydia's property. We don't want to give them anyone else to terrorize. And thank God you found it before it could lead them back to Erin's ranch."

He scraped a hand across his face. She was pretty sure her words hadn't swayed him.

"Maybe it was a good thing they put the tracker on. Maybe it was an answer to a prayer."

His eyes narrowed. "What now?"

She nodded, thinking it over. "If they hadn't put the tracker on, they wouldn't have followed us."

"Exactly." He said the word slowly, his confusion clear. "If I had been more vigilant, we wouldn't have almost just been run off the road."

She nodded. "Right. They wouldn't have flashed us, tried to kill us. But in doing so, they helped us solve the mystery of Lydia's death. I've been praying for an answer, Jesse. It's not as if the murderers were just going to walk up and tell me. But this—" she motioned to the shattered device "—this clarifies things."

"God works in mysterious ways?" Jesse asked, his tone wry.

She knew his words were laced with skepticism, but she said, "Yes. He does. Every single day."

He just looked at her, not even trying to conjure an argument.

"Now that that's taken care of," she said, "we really need to get moving again. It's already getting late."

"And it's going to get later still," Jesse said in exasperation. "We're close to our destination. Too close if they've been tracking us. I think we're going to have to find a more roundabout way to get there. I want to be sure we're not followed again."

Paige didn't argue. They had come too far to allow the thugs to catch up to them now.

Half an hour later, after Jesse was as convinced as could be that the killers weren't lurking around the next curve, they turned onto Bunchberry Lane. The road seemed to be in the middle of nowhere, but maybe that was because they'd looped around and had added some unnecessary back roads onto their journey.

It was a sparsely populated area with driveways placed great distances apart. Paige couldn't imagine her sister living this far out. Then again, Lydia had always loved lakes, so maybe that was a compromise she was willing to make.

Paige had suspected all along that Lydia had been killed, but there'd always been the possibility that she was wrong. What Jesse said made sense, though. She would have to ask Molly if she remembered bright lights. She didn't expect Molly to respond, but hopefully she could at least affirm with a nod of her head. She dreaded speaking to her niece about it, but it couldn't be helped. They needed as much information as they could get.

Jesse's GPS announced they were almost at their destination. It was later than Paige would like. Erin would be tucking Molly in right about now. Oh, how Paige wished she were there.

She hoped whoever owned this property was around. Not only that, she hoped they wouldn't be too irritated by their late arrival.

"This is it," Jesse said. He flipped on his blinker, though there wasn't another car in sight. He turned into the heavily wooded lot. His headlights sliced across a quaint two-story log cabin. To the right of it, set back into the woods, near the lake that shimmered like oil in the darkness, sat a smaller cabin.

"At least lights are on," she said, referring to the larger dwelling.

The words were only out of her mouth a second when the porch light flipped on.

"I suspect they don't get much company out this way." Jesse cut the engine. "Let's hope they're friendly folk."

They slipped from the truck, and Paige half expected the front door to fly open, since the occupants of the house obviously knew they'd arrived. The door remained closed, so the pair clomped up the steps.

Paige glanced at Jesse. His handsome face was illuminated in the soft glow of the light. She found herself, yet again, being so grateful for his presence. Just being near him soothed her.

"I think you should talk," he said gently. "If you don't mind. You might get farther than me. Since Lydia was your sister—"

"They might show me some sympathy," Paige surmised.

"Right." He knocked on the door.

Several long moments later, the door opened a crack. A security chain remained in place. A woman with silver hair peeked out at them.

"You aren't who I was expecting," she said, almost accusingly. "Can I help you with something?"

"I hope so," Paige said. She introduced herself and Jesse. "I have reason to believe my sister, Lydia Winslow, meant to rent from you."

"Oh." The woman gasped in surprise. "Lydia is your sister, you say?"

Paige nodded, relief spilling through her as she realized this woman knew her sister. They were on the right path. "She was."

"Was?" The woman allowed the door to creep open fully. "My name is Darlene. Would you like to come in?"

Paige and Jesse entered Darlene's house. She led them to her kitchen, where she motioned for them to have a seat at the table.

"Your sister…" Darlene began but let the question linger, as if afraid to finish the sentence.

"She—" Paige shifted in her seat. "She was killed in an accident a few weeks ago."

"Oh, my!" Darlene looked genuinely aggrieved. "I wondered what on earth happened to her. She seemed so determined to move in. Paid first and last months' rent without complaint." The woman clutched at her throat, clearly distraught. "I thought perhaps she was delayed. But since she'd already paid, we weren't too concerned."

"We?" Jesse asked.

"My husband, Allen, and I," she said.

"Is he home?" Jesse asked. "We'd like to ask you a few questions about Lydia if you don't mind. If he's around, it might be beneficial to get his take as well."

"I'm sorry," she said. "Friday is his night to go to town to play darts with the boys."

Under other circumstances, Paige would've smiled at that. Darlene was nearing seventy, and Paige had to assume her husband was as well.

"He won't be home for several more hours." She frowned. "I suppose you're here to collect her things."

"Her things?" Paige echoed. It hadn't occurred to her that Lydia may actually have brought her belongings here.

"Her SUV was filled to the brim, and she dropped everything off a few days after she paid rent," Darlene explained.

"Yes," Paige said. "I would like her things."

Darlene frowned. "I don't mean to be difficult, and you do look an awful lot like her, but do you have proof? I hate to ask, but I can't just let you take someone's belongings otherwise."

"We have proof," Jesse said. He pulled out his phone and pulled up Lydia's obituary. It was the best he could do. He showed it to Darlene.

"Oh, gracious," Darlene moaned. "That's just so sad. I heard there was a fatality on that awful road, but there was no name released. It never occurred to me that it was Lydia."

Paige rummaged around in her purse. "I also have this." She extracted her sister's will, the copy she had shown Bernadette the other day, and turned to the page that named her as the executor of Lydia's will.

Once that business was cleared up, Darlene said, "I can walk you over there."

"Actually," Jesse said, "could we ask you a few questions first?"

Darlene's brow furrowed. "That's right. You mentioned that earlier. What is it you want to know?"

"Did Lydia say why she was looking for a place to rent?" Jesse asked.

"Yes. She was quite candid," Darlene said. "She told me she was leaving her husband. She asked if she could pay cash, at least for the first few months, until her lawyer helped her straighten things out." The woman gave a sad smile. "She seemed like a nice enough lady. My husband and I rent the cabin out for extra income, to supplement our retirement. It didn't matter to us one way or another how she paid."

"She told you she was leaving her husband?" Jesse pressed.

"Yes." Darlene's gaze bounced between the two of them, landing on Paige. "You're her sister. You knew that, right?"

Paige cleared her throat. "Actually, I didn't. There are quite a few things that happened in the weeks before Lydia's death that have taken me by surprise."

"Did she elaborate?" Jesse asked. "Did she say why she was leaving him? Did she say anything about him?"

"I'm afraid not," Darlene admitted. "She seemed edgy. Sad. She didn't offer more, and I didn't feel it was my place to press. She said she had a little girl. Said she was looking forward to spending the summer here at the lake with her." Darlene gasped. "The girl?"

"She's all right," Paige said. "She was with Lydia, but she wasn't injured badly. She's with me now."

Darlene nodded. "I'm happy to hear that."

"Is there anything else you can think of that might be worth sharing?" Jesse asked. "Anything she said or did? Any questions she asked?"

"No," Darlene said. "I'm sorry. She called me in regard to an online ad I placed. She came out to check the cabin that same afternoon. Allen and I gave her a quick tour, and she said she'd take it on the spot. She paid. Allen gave her the key. We didn't bother with a lease," she said somewhat sheepishly. "The cabin was empty—our last renter moved out a month ago. We told her it was hers right away. She told us she didn't know when she'd be moving in officially, just that it would be soon. It was the next day that she showed up with her SUV full."

"She moved fast," Paige murmured, her eyes glistening.

"Did you talk to her that day?" Jesse asked.

"I didn't," Darlene said. "Most renters want their privacy. They aren't into chitchat. I always try to get a feel for that, but it takes a while. I was working in the flower bed when she came. She waved but didn't come over, so I let her be. She was busy with boxes. Took her about an hour. Then she hopped in her vehicle and drove away. That was the last time I saw her. I think it was about two weeks ago, maybe three. Like I said, she didn't commit to a move-in date, so I've been curious but not really concerned."

"Did she seem afraid to you?" Paige asked.

"Afraid?" Darlene's gaze narrowed. "I don't recall thinking that. I'd hate to speculate. Sometimes hindsight can play tricks on you, make you see something that wasn't there. As I mentioned, she was anxious." She leaned forward. "May I ask why all the questions?"

"Of course," Paige said. "My sister and I had drifted apart the last few years. When she died, no one knew where she was going. I simply wanted to piece together the last few weeks of her life. We found this address and thought we should check things out."

Paige did not want to tell this woman she thought Lydia was murdered. There was no point. Darlene had been very forthcoming. It appeared she had nothing else to share. Lydia's death was hard enough to discuss without bringing up the fact Paige thought she'd been killed.

"I understand that," Darlene said. "When we lose someone, it's natural to want closure."

"If there's nothing else you think you can share,"

Jesse said, "we'd really like access to the cabin so we can load up Lydia's belongings."

Darlene's chair ground across the linoleum as she slid backward. "Give me one second, and I'll fetch the spare key."

Jesse was a bit surprised that Lydia had wanted to stay here. While the cabin was spotless, it was old. Rustic. Very rustic. But if she thought her husband was trying to kill her, she probably really didn't care about decor. No. Safety had likely been the number one thing on her mind.

"That can't be all of her belongings," Paige said. She eyed up the dozen or so large boxes. "She must've left most of her things behind. I'm curious to see what she kept."

Paige glanced around the cabin. "I don't think this is really Lydia's taste, but I know she always wanted to live on a lake. I'm sure she was happy to be able to offer that to Molly." She paused, lost in thought, then said, "This seems like more of a retreat than a home."

"I was thinking the same thing," Jesse said. "I wonder if she was just going to stay here long enough to regroup, make a plan."

"That would make sense," she said. Her gaze met his. "She paid cash. She didn't want to be found. I know Darlene didn't want to speculate as to whether she was afraid, but it seems to me she may have been."

"Yes," he agreed softly, "you're probably right."

Paige shuddered. "It's been such a long day. Can we get these boxes loaded and get out of here? I'm anxious to see Molly. I know she'll be sleeping when we get home, but I just want to see her."

"Sure," Jesse said.

Darlene had let him back up to the cabin so he could just put his tailgate down and slide the boxes in. When the truck was loaded and the boxes were secured, Jesse went inside to return the key to Darlene. He thanked her for her time before returning to the truck.

Paige had started the engine. She had the radio playing softly in the background. When he opened the door, she was caught in the soft glow of the cab light. Even in her misery, she was beautiful. He found himself so drawn to her. He wanted to pull her into his arms, offer her support and maybe even affection. She looked so withdrawn, he didn't think she'd appreciate the gesture.

It was just as well.

He reminded himself he had no desire to start a relationship with her. Or with anyone. Although, he would admit that he no longer wondered if she was hiding something. He knew her fear was genuine, as was her desire to get to the truth. He wanted that for her. He wouldn't let this case rest until he was sure she was safe.

There was no denying he had feelings for her, but he decided they were feelings of friendship. Camaraderie. He'd never shared the story of how he'd come to live with the Coopers with anyone. It had always felt too personal. Yet he'd been able to share it with Paige with ease. Perhaps because she had bared her soul to him. She'd admitted her fears about losing Molly to Abe and confessed her sadness over the rift between herself and her sister.

They were both mentally worn, and the drive to the ranch was made in relative silence. The soft crooning of country songs floated from the radio.

When they arrived, the house was mostly dark, except for the entryway light that Erin had left on.

Though exhausted from an emotionally and physically grueling few days, they carried Lydia's boxes inside and neatly stacked them in the den, where Jesse slept.

"I should go through these now," Paige said when the last box was placed on the floor, "but I just don't think I can."

"We'll do it tomorrow," Jesse said, knowing the task was bound to be emotionally grueling. "I can take Molly and give you some privacy, or we can go through them together. Whatever is easier for you."

She nodded, her lips trembling and her eyes shimmering. He realized nothing he could do would make it easier for her. She pulled her gaze away from her sister's belongings. To Jesse's surprise, she closed the space between them and put her arms around him.

"Thank you," she said. "I don't even want to think of where I'd be right now without you."

He hugged her back, and they just stood there, wrapped in each other's arms, emotions swirling around them. When Paige looked up at him, he was sure he saw a flash of longing. The same longing that he was feeling.

Whether or not he wanted to admit it, he was falling for this woman. Falling for her steadfast determination to do what was right, for her loving heart that was so devoted to Molly. He was falling for her gentle spirit.

In that moment, he was lost in her.

Moving on instinct, he leaned down and kissed her. She returned the kiss with gentle purpose, letting him know that she wanted this, too. He let his lips linger, taking her in, but Gus groaned in the doorway, and

Jesse realized it would be all too easy for Molly or Erin to walk in.

He let Paige slip from his embrace. She sighed and moved away from him. Jesse didn't think it sounded like a happy sigh.

He winced. "I'm sorry. I should have asked first. I shouldn't have just—"

"No, it's not that," Paige said quietly. "It was a wonderful kiss."

"Then why are you frowning?" he asked.

"I like you. A lot, actually. I don't go around letting just anyone kiss me," she said with a small smile. But then her smile slipped. "I'm just not at a place in my life where it makes sense to start a relationship. Molly is going to need a lot of love and support. I need to focus on her. Not myself."

He nodded slowly. "I thought you were going to say we couldn't be together because we live too far apart, or that we've both worked hard to build our careers. Because as far as Molly goes, I'm getting kind of attached."

"I love my job," Paige said, "but it's not the center of my world. As for Molly, she's an easy child to love. That's why I need to put her needs first. We have so much going on right now. I already feel as if I'm being pulled in too many directions."

"I understand," he said and found that he did. Paige was devoted to her niece, and he would expect nothing less from her. "Maybe someday?" he asked, trying not to put too much pressure behind his words.

"Maybe someday," Paige said wistfully. "If we're meant to be together, it will happen. Nothing can stop God's plans for our lives."

He pulled in a breath, mulled her words over, then sighed. "You truly believe that, don't you?"

"With all my heart." She studied his face. "What do you believe, Jesse?"

What *did* he believe?

"I believe that there is a God, but I believe that maybe He likes some people more than others. Maybe He plays favorites," he said. "Gives them a better lot in life."

Paige's expression fell. "Do you really? Because I believe that God loves all of us. I don't think He plays favorites. I believe that free will, not just ours, but that of those around us, has ripple effects."

He thought about that for a moment. His mother leaving had caused a huge ripple effect. Truth be told, he often wondered about her past, her childhood. Had it been awful? What had formed her into being the person that she was? Maybe life's heartbreaks weren't really God's fault, as he sometimes used to think, but rather a compilation of man's free will. He raked a hand through his hair.

The thing was, Jesse couldn't stop thinking about his prayer up on Balsam Ridge Road. *Please, God.* Two words. So simple. More emotion than anything else. Did that even count as prayer? He didn't know but suspected it might. Then his mind backtracked to the prayer he'd sent up during their race through the woods. That had been a first for him.

Strangest of all, it was almost as if God had heard his call. Heard and answered his plea. Not just once, but twice. Was that possible? Would He even bother with a half-hearted believer?

He hadn't grown up in the faith. His mother, as far as he knew, had never set foot in a church. The Coopers had attended regularly. They'd dragged him along on occasion, but for the most part, they'd decided it was best if they didn't push their faith on him.

Ellen had always said it was something he would someday come to on his own. She'd been so sure. In fact, she'd confided that she even prayed about it. Knowing someone prayed for him was comforting.

He scrubbed his hand across his face. It suddenly all felt like too much to think about.

"Jesse?" Paige's voice was hesitant. "Are you okay? You looked like you were a million miles away right now."

He might as well have been, because he wasn't even sure where his mind had traveled.

"I'm fine," he assured her. The urge to tell her what he'd been thinking needled him, but now didn't seem like the time. He needed to examine his thoughts a bit more thoroughly, because her question—*What do you believe, Jesse?*—echoed through his mind.

A few weeks ago, he would've shrugged off the question. But now? The thought of his two scattered prayers skittered through his mind yet again. He *knew* that God had answered those prayers.

It was a humbling realization, and it left him a lot to think about.

ELEVEN

Paige stood propped against the kitchen door frame. Jesse had his back to her as he and Molly rolled a ball back and forth to the puppy. The pup would chase it, run over the top of it, then look at Molly as if asking what she should do next.

It warmed Paige's heart to see Jesse playing with her niece. The way Molly smiled at him gave her hope that she would break out of her shell soon.

She almost regretted rebuffing him last night. That kiss had been amazing. Just like Jesse. He was a remarkable man. He was kind, protective, devoted to his family. He was charming and clearly adored children. He rescued puppies. He was exactly the sort of man she could see herself spending the rest of her life with.

If only the timing were better, because it really could not possibly be worse. She had enjoyed being a single woman, volunteering at church, hanging out with friends. All while she patiently waited for the right man to come along. But now that Molly had landed in her life, she needed to do the responsible thing and put her own wants aside. At least for now, while Molly was still so vulnerable.

She loved her job, but she was sure she'd love being a librarian anywhere. There were other schools, other libraries. She liked Grand Junction, but Cascade Falls seemed like a lovely town. Smaller. Slower paced. A nice place to raise Molly. After only a few days, she felt a connection to Erin and would miss her when she and Molly went home.

And Jesse… Oh, how she would miss him. Her heart already ached at the thought of leaving him.

The puppy, apparently exhausted, dropped at Molly's feet. Molly smiled and scooped the little bundle into her arms, dropping kisses on the puppy's silky head. Jesse leaned over and gave the pup a gentle pat. Paige wasn't at all surprised when the name game began again.

"Petunia? Penelope? Pickles?" Jesse asked, putting some hope into the suggestions. "Tater Tot?"

Paige stifled a laugh while Molly blew out an exasperated sigh.

"Piper?" he pressed.

He received only an aggrieved look from Molly in reply.

"*Okay*, then," Jesse said. "Picking out names is not for wimps. I'm running out of ideas here, kiddo. I really wish you'd help me out."

"Still no progress on a name?" Paige asked, finally striding into the room. She gently ruffled Molly's hair. "It's just one small name. How hard can it be?"

He shrugged. "I'm starting to think we should just name her Little Puppy and be done with it." He was surprised when that, of all things, elicited a smile from Molly.

He arched a brow at her. "Is that it? Little Puppy?"

Molly laughed, a quiet but melodic sound. She shook her head.

Jesse theatrically threw his hands in the air. "What, then? I beg of you, tell me!"

Molly, still grinning, scrunched her face up as if thinking hard. Then she tapped her chin, as if lost in thought. Jesse and Paige shared a look and then both burst into quiet laughter. It was the first time Paige had seen this playful side of Molly. Perhaps her walls were finally starting to come down.

"You're thinking on it?" Jesse asked.

Molly nodded, her eyes twinkling.

"Do you have a name in mind?" Paige asked.

Molly nodded.

Jesse leaned forward, his eyes teasing and bright with anticipation. "Are you going to share?"

Molly shook her head, her eyes glinting with humor.

Gus padded into the room. Ignoring them, he slid under the edge of Molly's makeshift tent. She scooted toward the tent, clearly intending to follow.

Jesse shot Paige a look. She needed to talk to her niece about her mother's accident. Now didn't seem like a good time, but frankly, she couldn't imagine when a good time would be. They needed answers, and if Molly could provide any insight at all, it could help exponentially.

"Molly," Paige began, her voice gentle, "I need to ask you something."

The child looked at her expectantly.

"I don't want to make you think about sad things, but I have a very important question to ask you about the accident," Paige explained.

Molly looked down, snuggled the pup to her chest a little tighter, as if she knew what was coming.

"Sweetheart, right before the accident, do you remember seeing bright lights in the car?" She paused a moment, remembering how the cab of Jesse's truck had been awash with the glow. She had been immediately aware of the brightness but hadn't realized that they'd reflected back at Jesse, blinding him in the rearview mirror. "*Really* bright lights?" she pressed.

Molly's brow furrowed, her face scrunching as tears filled her eyes. Paige almost wished she could take back the question, but when Molly nodded vigorously, a gush of air whooshed from Paige. She wasn't sure if it was a reaction of surprise or relief.

"Is that when your mom said someone was trying to kill you?" Paige asked.

Molly nodded again, this time glancing at Paige with so much pain in her eyes it nearly broke Paige's heart.

There was one question burning through her mind. As much as she didn't want to ask, she had to. "Molly, in the hospital you said your mama said, 'He's trying to kill us.' Remember that?"

Molly seemed to cave in on herself. It seemed her full concentration was on the puppy, as if she was trying her best to ignore Paige.

"This is important, sweetheart. Did she say *who*? Did she name a name?" Paige's heart pounded. She glanced at Jesse for just a second. He looked as intense as she felt. For several long moments, Paige thought she wasn't going to answer.

Finally, she gave the subtlest of nods.

Paige pulled in a breath. In a voice as low and soothing as she could muster, she said, "Was it Abe?"

Without warning, Molly dived under the sheet, disappearing into the fort. They stood there a moment, frozen in shock.

It was Jesse who moved first, but Paige slid in front of him. She had started this. She needed to take responsibility. She dropped to her knees.

"Molly," she said softly, "I'm sorry I upset you." She lifted the edge of the sheet. Molly was sitting crisscross, petting the puppy, but she had her back to Paige. Gus was sprawled out on her other side. "I won't ask any more questions right now. Can you come out?"

Molly shook her head.

Paige put a hand on her shoulder, but Molly pulled away from her. Paige didn't think it was possible, but she felt her heart break just a little bit more. How could she make this right?

"Can I read you a story?"

No response.

"Should we find a movie? We can all watch it together."

Nothing.

"Would you like a snack? I saw some oranges in the kitchen."

Molly shifted the puppy but ignored Paige. Gus whined, and Molly scooted closer to him.

She felt Jesse's hand settle on her shoulder. She glanced back at him, letting the sheet fall. He nodded his head toward the kitchen.

She frowned, but he grabbed her hand and tugged her to her feet.

"Molly," Jesse said to her through the sheet, "Paige and I are just going to the kitchen. You give that little gal a few extra snuggles for us, okay? You know where to find us if you need us."

Still clutching Paige's hand, he led her away.

"Jesse," she grumbled under her breath, "I upset her. I need to make it right."

"Yeah? How?" he asked. "No offense, but it didn't seem to be working."

"There were lights, Jesse," Paige said, her voice quaking. "Just like we suspected. Someone forced Lydia off the road. Lydia told Molly who she thought was after them."

"I know," Jesse said gently. "I don't think you're going to get an answer from her right now. I think she needs some time to mentally decompress. Don't you feel that way sometimes? Like you just need a minute to yourself?"

"Of course," she agreed.

"I think kids need that, too. I've seen it in my job when kids get overwhelmed in stressful situations. They shut down. The more you press, the more withdrawn they get."

She nodded. "You're right. I work with kids, but she's family, and she's hurting. I feel like I'm abandoning her."

"I think the best thing for her right now is that little dog. They need each other." Jesse gave her a slight smile. "They're pretty attached to each other. You might want to reconsider bringing her home with you when this is all over. Little Puppy No Name might be the perfect therapy dog."

"I can't," Paige said on a half laugh. "I'm already struggling with Molly. I wouldn't have time for a puppy."

He shrugged. "We'll see."

Paige glanced toward the living room, where, of course, there wasn't a peep. Then she turned back to Jesse.

"I need to start going through those boxes," she said.

"I was just going to suggest that," he agreed.

Paige went to the tent and peeked inside, preparing to tell Molly that she would be in the den sorting through some things. When she lifted the sheet, she found Molly sound asleep and using Gus's belly as a pillow as he snoozed as well. The little beagle was curled up beside her. The puppy blinked her big brown eyes at Paige, then yawned and nestled her head against Molly's chest before drifting off to sleep.

Molly might be upset with her, but at least here at the ranch, she was able to find some comfort.

What were they going to do without this place?

The first three boxes they sorted through contained clothes. Two belonged to Lydia, the other to Molly, which would be useful. They removed every item from the boxes, just in case there was something tucked inside.

There wasn't.

The fourth box was heavier.

"Photo albums," Paige said. "I'd love to go through them when we have more time." For now, they sifted through everything, not sure what they were looking for and not finding anything that would help the case.

Jesse had thought things between him and Paige might be awkward after their kiss. Perhaps they had been for just a few minutes at breakfast. But the truth was, with Paige's and Molly's lives on the line, they both seemed willing to put any potential awkwardness aside and move forward.

Jesse moved the box of photo albums to the far side of the room where they'd placed boxes they had sorted through.

"Jesse?" Paige's voice shook.

He turned to face her where she sat on the edge of the sofa with another box opened at her feet.

"More photo albums?" he asked.

She nodded but then held up a stack of letters banded together. "But I also found these. They were on top of everything else." With a shaky hand, she untangled the rubber band. "The top letter is addressed to me."

Jesse dropped down on the couch next to Paige. "Did she write often?"

Paige shook her head. "Never." She flipped the envelope over, tearing the flap open, not noticing that two other pieces of mail had dropped to the floor. He picked them up as Paige began to read out loud.

"Dear Paige,
I'm writing this letter to tell you how much I miss you. You were right. I never should have married Abe. It has blown up in my face in the most horrendous way. I need some time to regroup. I have some decisions to make and need to spend some time alone. Just me and my little girl. But I'll be in touch soon. I hope with all of my heart that you can forgive me for shutting you out these past few years. I want to be close again, like we used to be. All of my love,
Lydia"

Paige clutched the letter to her chest, then clapped a hand over her mouth before a mournful sob broke free. Jesse took the letter from her and placed it on the end table. Paige slid into his arms, curling into his chest, and he held her as she cried.

"She loved you, Paige," Jesse said softly. "Just like you loved her."

"I know." Paige sniffled and reached for a tissue. "I wish we would have reconnected. I wish she would've come to me. I wonder what she meant when she said things had blown up with Abe."

"It could mean anything," Jesse said. It wasn't exactly incriminating. She could simply have been talking about his finances.

Paige nudged the box with her foot. "At least we have a bit more to go through. Maybe we'll still find something."

"Wait," Jesse said as Paige regained her composure and reached for a photo album. He twisted around and grabbed the two letters she'd dropped. "These fell when you were opening the letter from Lydia." He scanned the top envelope. "It looks like a credit card bill." He flipped to the last envelope and his pulse began to race. "Look at this, Paige." He held the envelope out so she could read her sister's swirly scrawl.

"It's addressed to a life insurance company," Paige said, her voice barely a whisper.

He handed it to her. "Open it carefully. Whatever is inside could be evidence."

Paige carefully tore the flap back. Her sharp inhalation warned him this might be what they were looking for. "It's the change-of-beneficiary form."

Jesse leaned over, scanning the page.

A quick perusal confirmed it was the very form that Bernadette had notarized. Lydia had officially changed the beneficiary of two million dollars from Abe Winslow to Paige Bennett.

"I think," Jesse said gruffly, "we found our motive. This was signed, dated and notarized three days before her death. I would say that once this reaches the insurance company, it'll be valid."

"What do I do with it?" Paige asked, her voice quaking.

"We'll hand it over as evidence for now," Jesse said. "But I'm sure we'll be able to scan a copy to the insurance company."

Paige nodded. "I don't really care about the money. I just don't want Abe to have it. Not after what he did. If the money goes to anyone, it should go to Molly."

Jesse carefully took the paper from her, folded it and put it back in the envelope. "I'll get this to the right person. I have to say, the evidence is starting to stack up against Abe."

His phone rang, and he tugged it out of his pocket. "It's Sheriff Sanchez," he said as he got to his feet.

"I'm going to check on Molly again," Paige said.

Jesse nodded to her even as he answered his phone with a brusque "Hello?"

Without preamble, the sheriff said, "We finally caught a break, and the last twenty-four hours have been pretty hectic."

"Twenty-four hours?" Jesse echoed. "And you're just touching base now?"

"Did you hear the part about things being hectic?" she asked lightly.

"Sorry," Jesse said, wincing. "I'm just anxious for news."

"You know we've been reviewing security footage from residents near Mr. Zielinski's office," she began.

"Yes." He wandered over to the window, but he was oblivious to the idyllic view.

"We didn't find anything useful until yesterday," she said. "The man who lives kitty-corner from the office was away on business. When he returned and heard about the murder, he contacted us. His footage is exactly what we've been waiting for."

Jesse's heart kicked in his chest. "What are you saying?"

"I'm saying, we got an ID for one of the men," Gloria said. "He escorted Rodney Zielinski from his office at approximately quarter after eleven Sunday morning. And by 'escorted,' I mean there's a very good chance he had a gun dug into the lawyer's side. You can't see it from the camera angle, but he walked a bit too close, his hand gripped around Zielinski's arm. Zielinski's Cadillac was parked across the street. There's only a few seconds of footage of him being led to the car, but it's enough. The guy's name is Marcus Cartwright. Cousin of Darci Cartwright, Abe Winslow's secretary. He's an auto mechanic. He's got a nice long rap sheet. Mostly misdemeanors and a few other charges that didn't stick."

"Sounds like he'd know how to cut Paige's brake lines," Jesse said.

"Exactly," the sheriff agreed. "There's another man, too, but he's wearing a ball cap pulled low, and we can't get a good look at his face."

"How was Cartwright identified?" Jesse asked.

"Joe Larson watched the tapes," she said, mentioning a deputy with the department. "He recognized Marcus because he's brought him in before. His official address is in Briarville, but he likes to commit his crimes away from home." Gloria paused a moment before saying, "He's definitely our guy. At least one of them. I'm just not convinced he's the mastermind."

"I think you're right about that." Jesse thought of Darci, his cousin. Was she the mastermind? Had she wanted Lydia out of the way so she could have Abe for herself? Or had she and Abe plotted together? "What about Darci? If she has a thing for Abe, maybe she was jealous enough to have Lydia killed."

"I'm getting to her," Gloria said. "We figured out she was the common link. Deputy Harris questioned her this morning. He said she was incredibly forthcoming. She positively ID'd Marcus even though we were already pretty certain. She claims Marcus is the black sheep of the family. Can't stay out of trouble. She said she doesn't spend much time around him but heard from another family member that he's been bragging about coming into a lot of money lately. We were able to corroborate that. He recently bought a Harley-Davidson. It was not cheap, and he paid cash."

"So who's paying him?" Jesse asked. "Is there any chance it's Darci? And she's just trying to throw us off her trail?"

"I don't think so," the sheriff said. "We've scoured her financials. She's doing all right, but there's nothing to indicate she has the means to pay anyone a substantial amount of money. Besides, if she was the one behind Marcus's actions, I think she'd be trying to steer us away from him. Not giving us the info we need."

True, Jesse thought.

"My mind keeps circling back to Abe Winslow," he admitted. He quickly updated the sheriff on the form he and Paige had just found. "Abe could've known that Paige was set to get the money, not him. Maybe Darci talked about her cousin being a criminal, and he tracked the guy down, offered him a cut to get Paige out of the way. With Paige dead, she sure couldn't inherit the settlement."

"It's possible. And hopefully, we'll know soon. Darci directed Chad to the auto shop where Marcus works, but his boss said he hasn't shown up this week. Didn't call, just didn't show."

"Probably because he came into a windfall," Jesse muttered.

"I'm sure you're right. Darci also said Marcus spends most nights at Shady's Bar. We'll have someone posted there as well as at his house. We'll get him," she said assuredly. "Now that we know who we're looking for, it's just a matter of time."

"Can I do anything to help?" Jesse asked.

"Yes. Continue to keep Paige safe. I'll keep you posted on the rest."

The phone went dead in his ear.

He turned away from the window to find Paige standing in the doorway of the den.

"What's going on?" she asked, brow furrowed in concern.

Jesse reiterated everything he'd learned.

By the time he'd finished, Paige had slumped against the door frame. She closed her eyes and rubbed a hand against her forehead. She looked utterly exhausted. He strode over to her, rubbed his hand gently down her arm. When her eyes fluttered open, he wanted to fall right into those beautiful blue depths.

"It's going to be okay," he said.

She looked at him with so much trust in those lovely cornflower eyes. For just a moment, she hesitated. Then she nodded. "You're right. I know you are. I'm so anxious for this to be over. It's almost hard to believe that there's finally been a break in the case. It's a lot to take in." On a half laugh, half sob, she said, "I can't believe we have Darci Cartwright to thank for helping everything come together."

He reached for her, and she slipped into his arms, just as she'd slipped right into his heart. His instincts told him this would come to a close soon, but so would his time with Paige. He closed his eyes, held her close and dreaded how quickly their time together was going to come to an end.

TWELVE

Paige tried to relax into the sofa. Jesse had set up a game of checkers on the coffee table in front of her. He was teaching Molly how to play. The two were almost comical as they good-naturedly plotted against one another. Erin was curled up in her recliner on the other side of the room. She must've realized Paige wasn't in the mood for chitchat and had submerged herself in a novel.

Paige couldn't stop thinking about Marcus Cartwright. How had he gotten involved? Had he killed Lydia? Because now she knew beyond a doubt that her sister was murdered. Had Abe paid him? That was what it was beginning to look like.

Sheriff Sanchez had texted some pictures to Jesse. Paige didn't recognize either man, and she couldn't say if they were the men on the beach. As expected, the shot of Marcus Cartwright was clear, easy to make out. The other man appeared to be shorter, stockier, and could definitely be the man who'd chased them through the woods. Though there was no way to prove that with the photo the sheriff sent. Unlike the leather jacket the man was wearing in the woods, this guy was wearing denim, but he did have something glinting in his ear. It was visible just past the brim of the ball cap that covered his face.

Her sister's letter was forefront in her mind as well. Just a few short sentences, yet they were everything to Paige. They showed her Lydia's heart, let her know that her sister loved her. If only she had been able to speak with her one last time, to tell Lydia she loved her, too. She had to assume that her sister knew.

Blowing out a calming breath, she forcefully pushed all her stressful thoughts aside and began reciting her favorite Bible verses over and over in her mind. It was a tactic she often used when feeling overwhelmed. Just as her heartbeat began to calm, her phone rang, and she nearly leaped off the couch in surprise.

Since being at the ranch, she'd received so few phone calls. Other than Bernadette, a couple of her friends had called to check on her, but she'd been brief with them, not wanting to divulge what was going on. She glanced at her phone now but didn't recognize the number.

Jesse glanced up from the game.

"Hello?" Paige answered.

"Is this Paige Bennett?"

The voice was female and unfamiliar.

"It is," she replied.

"This is Darci." There was a moment of hesitation before she continued with, "Darci Cartwright. I work for Abe?" The last came out sounding like a question. "I found your number scribbled on a notepad in his desk."

"Yes, of course, Darci," Paige said, briefly wondering why the woman was poking around in Abe's desk. Jesse's gaze flew to her face. "I know who you are. Is there something I can help you with?" Paige couldn't imagine why the woman was calling her, but it seemed the polite thing to say.

"No. But I think I can help you," Darci said.

"From what I've heard, you've helped quite a lot already," Paige replied. "I can't tell you how grateful I am."

"I'm really sorry about your sister," Darci said softly. "I didn't know her well. She didn't come into the office often, but when she did, she was always nice to me."

"Thank you," Paige said.

"That's why I need to see you," Darci went on. "When I was filing some paperwork this afternoon, after I spoke to that cop, I found something."

"What?" Paige asked as dread began to pool in her stomach.

"It's better if I show you," Darci said. "Give me your address, and I'll bring it to you."

Paige winced. "I can't do that."

"Why not?" Darci demanded. "I thought this was important to you."

For just a moment, Paige forgot how grateful she was for the girl's help. All she could think of was the way she'd seemed so haughty and unpleasant when they'd visited Abe's office.

"It is important—it's just…" What could Paige say? That she was in hiding and didn't want to give away her location? She wasn't sure how much Darci knew about the current situation, but she could hardly admit that.

"Okay," Darci said, drawing out the word in a way that sounded as if she thought Paige was ungrateful for not accepting her offer. "Do you want to come to me?"

Paige frowned. "Why didn't you just call Deputy Harris?"

Jesse did a masterful job of paying attention to Molly and the game they were playing while clearly eavesdropping on Paige's conversation. Not that she minded. She wanted his guidance.

"No offense, but I'm not a fan of cops," she said. "Besides, maybe it's nothing. I could be overreacting. I don't want to involve the police if I'm wrong. It would be *so* embarrassing. I'd rather talk to you in person."

"I'm not sure I can meet you in person," Paige said. She hated the thought of leaving Molly with Erin yet again, even if the woman didn't seem to mind. Having heard the one-sided conversation, Erin slid from the chair and silently shooed Jesse away from the game of checkers. She smiled and whispered something to Molly. Molly nodded, and Jesse got to his feet. He quickly moved to Paige, and she tilted the phone toward him.

Darci blew out a breath. "All right. Forget I called. It's probably nothing. I'm sorry I bothered you."

Let's go, Jesse mouthed.

"Wait!" Paige said. Though there was no convenient way to handle this situation, she couldn't let possible evidence slip through their grasp. "I was in the middle of something," she said to stall for a moment. It was true; she'd been watching a game of checkers and reciting Bible verses. "But I could be at your house in… say an hour? Would that work?"

She didn't want to give away her location, but it would take about that long to get to Briarville.

"That's fine. Come alone," Darci requested. "I don't want to talk to that deputy again."

Paige could understand that. Whether you were innocent or guilty, being questioned by law enforcement was bound to make anyone anxious. She knew she'd been anxious the day Sheriff Sanchez had questioned her, and she hadn't done anything wrong either.

Jesse pointed at himself.

"I'll come to you," Paige said, "but I'm not coming alone. I'm going to bring Jesse with me."

"Who's Jesse?" She groaned. "Oh, you mean the guy who almost got himself run over in the parking lot?" she asked with barely disguised disdain.

Jesse grumbled something under his breath, and Paige arched a brow.

"Fine," Darci continued. "Bring him if you have to. Do you have a pen handy?"

Jesse scrambled to find her a pen and paper. Then she quickly scribbled down Darci's address.

With a quick goodbye to Molly and Erin, Paige and Jesse hustled out the door.

"What could she have found in Abe's office?" Paige wondered as they bumped down the gravel driveway.

"You heard what she said. Maybe it's nothing," Jesse offered. "I don't want to get too excited."

Paige clenched and unclenched her hands. An overwhelming feeling of dread crept over her. She told herself she and Jesse were fine. They were only running what amounted to an errand. Marcus and his accomplice would be caught soon. Police were watching for Marcus at his house and his favorite hangout.

Soon. He'd be caught *soon.*

Still, the feeling of foreboding lingered.

Could this finally be what they needed? Could Darci have information that would lead to Lydia's killer? Would she and Molly be safe? Though it had only been a few weeks since she'd first realized someone was after her, she could barely remember what it felt like to live a normal, quiet life.

Her gaze slid across the truck to Jesse, and he managed a reassuring smile for her. Would he be a part of that life?

Jesse had confirmed the address Darci had given was truly hers. After circling the block twice, looking for any suspicious vehicles, he swung into her driveway. He noted that her house was small, and it looked cozy with dangling flowers and wicker furniture on the porch. It was located in a quiet neighborhood on the edge of town. Thin rows of trees on either side of the house offered a modicum of privacy. The garage jutted out from the house, and a pathway curled around the length of the garage, leading to the front door.

When he and Paige slid from the truck, he heard the unmistakable twang of country music pulsing from inside. He thought it was a good thing it was so early in the year. With the air so chilled, the neighbors all had their windows shut, so her music likely didn't bother them.

The house was only one level, and all of the lights appeared to be on. Either the girl didn't care one iota about the environment, or she was feeling a bit on edge. He was guessing it was maybe a bit of both.

"She sure likes her music loud," Paige noted as they rounded the garage and strode up the sidewalk.

"I'd say," Jesse agreed. He glanced over his shoulder out of habit. All was clear.

Paige rang the doorbell.

A moment later, the music was turned down. Darci opened the door. Her dark hair was scooped into a messy bun on the top of her head. She wore yoga pants, an oversize T-shirt, and held a pint of ice cream with a spoon protruding from it.

"I was wondering if you'd ever get here," she said.

"Here we are," Jesse said lightly, knowing they'd made good time and had arrived within the hour, as promised.

"This way," Darci said once they were inside. The music still spilled from some unseen source, but at least the volume was tolerable.

They followed her to the kitchen. She opened the freezer and stuck her dessert, spoon included, inside. Then she spun around and grabbed a manila envelope off the counter. She held it in the air triumphantly.

"What is it?" Paige asked, her tone polite but overtly curious.

Darci tipped the envelope upside down. Confetti spilled out.

Was this some kind of joke? Jesse wondered.

"Shredded papers," Paige said flatly. "You brought us over for that?"

Darci huffed at them, as if she couldn't believe how clueless they were.

"It's not just *any* paper. I've always loved jigsaw puzzles," she said as she peeked inside the envelope and pulled a full sheet of paper out, "but this took forever to put together."

Jesse imagined it had stayed inside the envelope due to all of the tape stuck to it.

Darci handed the paper to Paige with a proud flourish.

"What is it?" Paige scanned the page and gasped. Her eyes lifted to his. "It's divorce papers. It looks like Lydia had them drawn up."

"Part of the papers, anyway," Darci corrected. "I managed to piece together the front page." She motioned to what was *not* confetti on the counter. "I'll leave the rest to you."

"You found these in Abe's office?" Jesse clarified.

"Yes. I heard him shouting the day you visited. I heard him say Lydia wasn't leaving him. But clearly—" she waved a hand their way "—she was. And he knew it. I'm not sure if he ripped the papers up when he got them or just recently. But he was obviously lying."

"And you just stumbled across them?" Paige asked.

"Of course not," Darci said, sounding indignant. "I had to go snooping."

Jesse steepled his fingers together, then pressed them to his lips. This woman was something else. Young and impetuous, yet oddly helpful.

Paige cleared her throat. "Forgive me for saying so, but I got the impression you're rather, um, fond of Abe."

Darci snorted indelicately. "That was before I realized he tangled my cousin up in an awful mess. And *certainly* before I realized he probably killed Lydia." She winced, showing uncharacteristic chagrin. "Sorry, Paige. I didn't mean to blurt that out."

Paige waved the words away with her hand.

"Where did you find the papers?"

"I'd rather not say," Darci announced. "I don't want to incriminate myself. Like I said, I don't know if it's useful, but I thought I'd let you decide. At the very least, it proves Abe is a *liar.*" She scowled, as if she could think of nothing worse.

He *had* lied to them. But it wasn't as if he had lied under oath. While the papers solidified that Abe was hiding things, it wasn't a crime to tear up papers.

"Thank you," Paige said.

"There's more," Darci added.

"More papers?" Paige asked.

Darci shook her head. "No. I mean, I have more information. I didn't want to share it with the deputy that was here earlier. He was *cute*, but he was *rude*."

Jesse swallowed a scoff. He doubted Chad had been rude. He'd likely been blunt, just doing his job. Jesse had never met a person, innocent or guilty, who actually enjoyed being questioned.

Ignoring her comment, Paige asked, "What information?"

"I don't want to go to the cops with this, in case I'm mistaken," Darci admitted, looking legitimately concerned. "But if I'm right, it would be wrong to keep it to myself."

Jesse realized she clearly had no idea who he was. To her, he was just a guy who tagged along with Paige. A guy who'd almost gotten himself run over in the parking lot. He thought it prudent to keep it that way. He wouldn't lie, but he certainly wasn't going to volunteer the information.

"The deputy showed me a picture they'd taken off some security footage. I recognized Marcus right away. The other guy, well, I wasn't so sure about him. At first, I didn't think I knew him, and I told Deputy Harris so. But I haven't been able to get the picture out of my head. You can't see the guy's face. But his size and the way he carried himself was kind of familiar."

Jesse's heart seemed to flip in his chest. Could she really know the identity of the second gunman? The one who'd chased them through the woods?

"Go on," he gently urged.

"It's a small town," Darci continued with a shrug. "When I go out with my friends, sometimes we run into Marcus. There's this guy he hangs out with." She paused, seemed to mentally backtrack. "See, this is why I didn't want to talk to the deputy. What if I'm wrong? I don't want to cause problems for him. He seems like a nice guy, just a little on the quiet side. I've heard rumors he and Marcus are in cahoots. Thick as thieves, if you will. Marcus tends to do that to people. He draws them in."

Jesse let her prattle on a few more moments, afraid if he interrupted her, she'd change her mind completely, and they *needed* this information.

"How about if I check this guy out?" Jesse asked. "There's no need to involve Deputy Harris." Though he would pass the information along to Sheriff Sanchez.

"You'd do that?" she asked.

"Sure," Jesse said, feigning patience. "What's the guy's name?"

"Charlie Wilson." She frowned. "No, Wilkinson? I think that's it." She nodded to herself. "Yup. That's it. Wilkinson."

Jesse restrained his sigh of relief. He didn't want to give too much away, but he wanted to whoop for joy now that they had a second name.

"That's very helpful," he said calmly. "And I assure you, you have nothing to worry about. If this Charlie Wilkinson is innocent, nothing will come of it. But if he is guilty, you may have just helped catch a killer."

"Is there anything else you would like to share?" Paige asked.

"Nope," Darci said. "I think I've done enough good

deeds the past few days to last me a lifetime. This crime solving is all very stressful."

Jesse gave her a tight smile.

"We should go," Paige said, taking his hand and tugging him toward the door. "Darci, we appreciate your help so very much. It's getting late, and I'm sure you'd like to settle in for the night. I'd like to be home in time to tuck Molly in."

"Oh. Right, of course. What a sweet girl." Darci flashed a genuine smile. "I'll miss seeing her around."

She led them to the door and ushered them outside, but she made no promises when Jesse asked her to let them know if she came up with anything else.

As they walked down the sidewalk, he made a mental plan. He'd call Sheriff Sanchez as soon as he reached the truck to let her know about Charlie Wilkinson. He'd take Paige back to the ranch and then head into the department so he'd have more resources at his disposal. He'd see what he could find out about the man. Maybe they'd even be able to apprehend the guy tonight. He assumed Marcus Cartwright was still at large, or he'd have been notified.

Music boomed from behind them. Jesse glanced back, not surprised Darci had cranked the volume up already. When he spun back around, he realized instantly that there was a problem. He reached for his gun the second he noticed two men silhouetted in the dim glow of twilight. They had just stepped around the side of the garage. Dread sprinted through his veins as he realized the men had been waiting for them. He was not going to be able to move fast enough. Still, he tried to dart in front of Paige and take aim at the men, but he was too late.

"Gotcha." Marcus's voice was cold, but the jolt of electricity that tore through Jesse's thigh was white-hot. The probes of a Taser had easily pierced his jeans, embedding in his flesh.

He heard Paige cry out as the other man tased her. He tried to fight against the current jolting through him, his only thought that he needed to protect Paige, but the voltage was too strong. He was vaguely aware of tumbling to the ground…hitting the concrete sidewalk…seeing Paige fall…wondering if Darci had set them up.

As he lay there trying to catch his breath and regain his faculties, he realized the garage provided coverage on one side, bushes on the other. Darkness was falling, and he doubted any of the neighbors were outside this gloomy evening. Darci's music would drown out the sound of their struggle. He was helpless, and it was a feeling he loathed.

"We got 'em, Charlie!" Marcus growled, his voice a disconcerting blend of exuberance and malice. "We finally got 'em!"

Jesse heard Paige whimper. He tried to move and was able to roll over. He hoped to get to his knees, but Marcus kicked him in the ribs, and he went down again. At the sound of Paige's cry, Charlie backed up. He threw his hands in the air.

"I don't like this," he said to Marcus. "I don't like this at all! You told me we were just going to talk to Darci, not do…do *this*! I'm out!" He spun and took off running.

Feeling started creeping back into Jesse's legs, and he was sure he'd regain his ability to fight, even if weakly, any second now. But before that could happen, Marcus knelt down next to him, a sneer on his face. He plastered a damp rag over Jesse's mouth and nose, and Jesse's consciousness swirled away.

THIRTEEN

Nausea rolled through Jesse in not-so-gentle waves. The cloying taste in his mouth nearly made him gag. His eyes were gritty and his eyelids heavy, but he managed to pry them open. The moment he did, realization speared through him. The memory of what had transpired whipped through his mind.

They had been attacked, drugged.

Bright industrial lights glared from above. He was sitting on a cold concrete floor. A hard metal beam ran the length of his back. His hands were behind him, secured to the beam. Not tied with rope, though, he realized almost immediately. He was restrained with something plastic. A zip tie? Yes, that was what it was. His feet were free, but they weren't of much use at the moment.

He swung his head to the right and regretted it as pain slammed into his brain.

"Jesse," Paige muttered from several feet away. Her voice was raspy, her eyelids droopy. She was restrained, tied to a support beam, just as he was. She was pale, her expression wary.

He blinked hard, trying to clear the blur from his eyes. "Where are we?"

"A warehouse, I think." She motioned with her head. "This must be where they store their equipment."

Jesse quickly assessed the situation. Moment by moment, he became more alert, scanning his surroundings, trying to absorb what he saw. Work trucks, Bobcats and other small machinery filled the space. A logo on the side of a work truck boasted Hearth & Home Construction.

He yanked at his restraints. They were tight, leaving no wiggle room. That didn't stop him from continuing to try. He tugged and squirmed. Maybe he could break the restraints. Or maybe he could maneuver enough to get a hand free. There were two large garage doors. Off to his left, much closer to them, was a regular entrance door. How could he get them free and out of the building? It was bad enough he was here, but he couldn't tolerate the idea of anything happening to Paige.

Please, God, please help us. I know I haven't been faithful, he began. *I want another chance to do better, to be better. I want a chance at a life with Paige, and Molly, too. Please, help us out of this.*

A door opened from a side office he hadn't noticed. Abe's business partner, Susan, strode toward them wearing a scowl and toting a handgun.

"It's about time the two of you woke up. You've kept me waiting far too long."

"You?" Jesse grated out. "It was you behind this?"

"Surprise," she said, her tone flat. "You two have caused me *so* much trouble. Even though this is hardly how I want to spend my evening, imagine my delight when Marcus let me know he had the two of you bound and gagged."

Jesse's head whipped around. "Where's Darci? Is she in on this?"

Susan scowled. "That meddling little nuisance? Of course not. She's safe. For now. But Marcus will be having a word with her soon enough about the virtues of family loyalty. She'll either need to agree to keep her mouth shut, or Marcus will have to come up with a more permanent solution. Although, it did work to our advantage that she's such a blabbermouth. Because when Marcus went to have a little chat with her tonight, he found the two of you."

Jesse was relieved Darci hadn't betrayed them and was safe for the time being.

"Does Abe know what you've done?" Paige demanded. Her voice was strong, clear, though Jesse knew she had to be as worried as he was. "Is he part of this?"

"How delightful that you think so. That means my plan was a success," Susan said, her eyes sparkling. "Abe looks guilty, but he's not, so they will never be able to tie anything to him."

"It'll never work." Jesse smirked. "Your guys left a trail of clues, lady. You really aren't that smart." Erin knew the last place they had gone was Darci's house. As soon as she realized they weren't coming home, she'd call the sheriff. Surely there would be sign of the attack at Darci's? But would anyone figure out where they'd been taken before it was too late?

Jesse's sass earned him a smack across the cheek with the butt of Susan's gun. He winced, biting back a groan, not wanting her to know it set sparks off behind his eyelids.

Paige gasped and began struggling against her bind-ings. "You are not going to get away with this."

"Oh, but I am," Susan said. "We're working on a new house right now. A beautiful monstrosity up in the hills. We're getting ready to pour the cement foundation." She paused, flashing them a pleased smile. "With some help from Marcus, your bodies will be buried, and no one will ever think to look for you there."

Jesse's blood turned to ice. Buried under the foun-dation of a new home? Covered in concrete? She was right—no one would ever look for them there.

Susan took a step away from him, concentrating on Paige now. "Where's the life insurance policy? With all of the digging you two have been doing, you must've found it by now."

Paige tilted her head, mustering a confused expres-sion. "Life insurance policy? What policy?"

Jesse continued to tug at the restraints. He felt his skin tear. His blood began to trickle down his wrists. He didn't feel any pain, only intense determination to get out of here. Perhaps the blood would help him slide free of his binds.

"Don't play dumb with me," Susan barked. She took a step closer, waving her gun at Paige. "I know Lydia signed papers to take Abe off the policy. I know—"

"What is this?" Abe Winslow's voice echoed in the cavernous space as he stormed into the warehouse through the side door.

Paige sucked in a terrified gasp, but Jesse realized the man looked absolutely horrified by what he saw. Abe's keys dangled from his hand as the door slammed shut behind him. His gaze scanned Paige and Jesse, and his complexion paled. "What have you done?" he asked Susan, his voice hoarse.

She blinked at him a few times, as if trying to comprehend that he was really here. "Abe... I...I'm trying to *help* you."

"Help me?" he asked in disbelief. He rushed toward Jesse, as if completely oblivious that his business partner was wielding a weapon. "I got a phone call. Some guy told me something criminal was going down at the warehouse. I thought it was a prank, but I felt obligated to check it out," Abe muttered.

Charlie. Jesse thought of the wild look in the man's eyes before he'd taken off. Hope surged through him, because if he was not mistaken, Abe had played no part in this treachery. In fact, it seemed he was here to help.

"Get away from him!" Susan shrieked.

Jesse felt Abe's hands go still around his wrists.

"Susan," Abe said, his tone calming, "you don't want to do this."

"I said get away from him," she demanded again. When he hesitated, she swung the gun, aiming at Paige's chest. "Get away, or I'll kill her."

"Put the gun down," Abe urged. "I'll step away."

Jesse tried not to flinch in surprise when he felt Abe shove something into his hand. The man then moved around him, ignoring him as he edged slowly toward Susan.

Jesse fingered the object. Abe's key chain. He felt the rough edge of a key. Could he use it to cut himself free? He would have to.

Wait, he thought as his finger edged along something else. *What is this?* His heart leaped as his thumbnail caught on a ridge of metal. Carefully, he tugged at it.

Thank You, Lord! The small blade of a Swiss Army knife popped open.

He glanced at Paige. Her eyes were wide. From her vantage point, she could see what he was up to, and she quickly glanced away, obviously not wanting to draw attention to him.

While Susan was preoccupied with Abe, he twisted enough to be able to saw through the plastic confining him.

"Susan," Abe said calmly, holding his hands out to the side as if in supplication, "what is going on here?"

"You are not supposed to be here," she grated out, as if that was the only problem with this situation.

Abe scrubbed a hand over his face. "I think you better start talking."

"It's not my fault things turned out this way!" She pointed the gun toward Paige. "You were not supposed to get custody of Molly." She swung back to pout at Abe. "Those idiots I hired messed everything up."

Her expression was pinched, her eyes wild. She looked like a woman on the edge. The edge of completely losing it.

"I had everything worked out so perfectly," she told Abe. "I knew you were skimming money from the business. So much money," she said woefully. "And I wanted to help you."

"What?" Abe asked, sounding bewildered.

"I had it all planned out," Susan said, more to herself than anyone else. She began to pace while still wielding the gun.

Jesse tried not to squirm too much as he maneuvered. It wasn't easy. The zip ties were tight, and getting the blade tilted at the right angle was a challenge.

The blood coursing down his wrists made his fingers slick. It would be all too easy for the blade to slip from his precarious grip. That would be disastrous. He concentrated on what he was doing while still half listening to what Susan was saying.

She explained that, over a year ago, she'd talked Lydia into taking out a life insurance policy on herself. Given that her first husband had died and left her nearly destitute, it hadn't been hard. She had wanted Molly to be cared for should something happen to her. Because she was estranged from her sister, and because Molly was so young, it only made sense for her to name Abe as the beneficiary.

"I bided my time, though," Susan said proudly. "I couldn't let the timing be too suspicious."

Meanwhile, she began to make Lydia question her marriage. She hinted that Abe was having an affair with Darci. It was easy to believe, because anyone could see the secretary had a crush on the man. A rift grew between Lydia and Abe. The rift had pushed Abe and Susan closer, just as she'd hoped. She continued to fill Lydia's head with lies about Abe, making up stories about their youth to the point that Lydia began to fear him. She'd painted him as having a violent, vindictive side and convinced Lydia that Abe was unstable and an unfit husband.

"I did it for you, Abe. There was so much at stake. It was the only way out of the financial mess you created for us," Susan said, her voice trembling, her eyes begging him to understand. "I did it for you. It should have all fallen into place so perfectly. I was going to release you from a loveless marriage. You were supposed to turn to *me* for comfort once *she* was gone. We were supposed to raise Molly together. *We* were supposed to be a family. The insurance policy was just the icing on the cake. We were supposed to use it to save the business," Susan lamented. "It was the perfect plan."

"Oh, Susan," Abe said regretfully.

"You had to have known that I've been in love with you since we were young. I can love you the way you deserve. I was supposed to help you save our company!" she cried. "But Lydia messed everything up! She decided to leave you, like I knew she would, but the day she left, she confided in me that she'd created a will and changed the policy. I thought she would've forgotten about it."

Jesse thought he knew why Lydia had made the changes. This woman had pushed too hard, had driven Lydia too far away from Abe. But Susan had been too blinded by her obsession to see that.

Susan ran a hand through her hair, her expression crumpling. "Her crash looked like an accident. I knew that if you did become a suspect, nothing could be traced back to you because you were innocent. Don't you see? I was protecting you." She pulled in a few ragged breaths. "I planned everything out so perfectly. But when she told me she changed the beneficiary but hadn't had a chance to mail it, I knew I had to find it!"

"Did you kill Lydia's lawyer?" Abe asked, his tone shaky.

"Of course not," Susan scoffed. "I hired that nitwit Marcus Cartwright to do it. Darci was always prattling on about how her cousin couldn't stay out of trouble. I was sure he'd do whatever I asked for the right amount, but the man is utterly incompetent."

Not that incompetent, Jesse thought. He had managed

to kill Rodney Zielinski. He was beginning to see that only by the grace of God had he and Paige been spared.

"Why?" Abe demanded. "Why have him killed?"

Her lips trembled, and she looked bereft. "Well, I didn't *want* to, but Lydia told me she had the form notarized at her lawyer's office. I thought he had a copy, but he didn't. Once I knew that, it wasn't as if Marcus and that friend of his could just walk away. Zielinski would've called the police. They had to do *something*."

"*You* killed my sister," Paige grated out.

"As she was getting ready to leave town, she called me," Susan said sulkily. "That's when she admitted she'd changed her life insurance and written up a will. I was on my way home, and it didn't take me long to head in her direction. I followed her when she left town. I just wanted to know where she was going, but she wouldn't tell me. She told me it was better if no one knew, but I knew I had to keep track of her, had to be able to get to her." She paused as if remembering that night, then said, "I realized how winding the road was, how dangerous. I flipped my high beams on, and—" she shrugged as if it were no big deal "—over the edge she went."

Abe let out a strangled sound as he pressed a fist over his mouth.

"It was a terrible decision," she said more to herself than anyone else. "I should not have deviated from the plan. I eliminated her too soon. It simply complicated *everything*. I shouldn't have acted until I knew precisely where that policy was, but I was worried that if I waited too long, she would mail it. It was a conundrum. Kill her without knowing where the form was, or wait and risk it being sent off? Do you know *why* she hadn't mailed it yet? She told me she'd run out of stamps." Susan laughed, as if that was the most absurd thing in the world.

Jesse realized then that the small stack of mail they'd found had all been devoid of stamps. So that was why they hadn't been sent. He could only imagine how busy Lydia had been during her last days, packing, planning her escape. A trip to the post office should have been a priority, but apparently it hadn't been.

"I assumed she had it in the vehicle with her, but I checked. We were the only two on the road. I thought if a car came by, I'd pose as an innocent bystander who saw her go over. But no one came. I expected there to be moving boxes and luggage. But all I found was her purse. The beneficiary form wasn't there. I knew then that I had a problem," Susan admitted.

Jesse clenched his teeth. No one had known Susan had been there. He'd read the report. He knew a young couple had eventually seen Lydia's taillights glowing down the hill. They'd made their way to the car after calling for help. Then the scene had been descended upon by rescue workers. No one had suspected a crime until later, and by then, the place had been trampled.

"You almost killed my niece," Paige accused.

"That was also not my fault," Susan said forcefully. "Abe mentioned Molly was supposed to be at a friend's house that night. How was I supposed to know that Lydia had changed the plan? How was I to know she was in the car? You can imagine my surprise when I saw Molly, unconscious in the back seat. If her daughter was injured, she only had herself to blame."

Paige's anger simmered beneath the surface. How she longed to be free. She wanted to face this madwoman head-on, not while sitting on the ground tied to a pole.

Susan's gaze sliced to Jesse, and Paige realized his movements must've nabbed her attention. He wasn't free yet, and Susan's interference just wouldn't do. She had to distract the woman.

"What are you saying?" Paige asked. "It sounds to me like you're in love with a man who stole from you."

"He wasn't embezzling," Susan said. "He was borrowing. He meant to pay it back someday."

"I did," Abe said earnestly. "But now I see that my gambling was out of control."

Forgetting about Jesse, Susan turned her attention to Abe.

"You almost *destroyed* our business. But am I *angry* with you? No! I *love* you! Don't you see?" Susan's lips trembled. "I've always loved you. But you've never thought of me as anything more than a little sister."

"Yes," Abe said quietly. "I do see. I see now how much you love me. How you have for years. I'm sorry. So sorry it's taken me so long. I don't know how I missed what was right in front of me."

"Do you know how hard it was to have to pretend to like her when she took *everything* from me?" Susan cried.

Paige bit back a scream of anger. This woman had pretended to be Lydia's friend. She had conned her, misled her. She'd used her. Then she'd killed her.

"She had everything I have ever wanted, and did she appreciate it? No! She didn't deserve you," Susan grated out. "I knew that if I could get Lydia out of the way, I could be there for you. I could be your rock. I could help you to see that we are meant to be together."

"I understand," Abe said. He nodded, as if encouraging her to believe him. "I get it. Through the years, you've always been there. It's not that I thought of you as a little sister." He flashed Susan a wistful smile. "It's the opposite, actually. I thought you were a beautiful woman who was so far out of my league that I'd never stand a chance with you. It's not too late. You and I can still have it all."

Susan paused, studying his face.

"We can raise Molly together," she said, her voice filling with hope. "I know you love her. I love her, too. I was supposed to be her mother after Lydia was gone. We were supposed to be a family, but nothing went how it was supposed to. Molly was supposed to go to you. Not *her*! I had to destroy the beneficiary form, and I had to get *her* out of the way. Don't you see?"

"Sure," Abe said soothingly. "Sure. It all makes sense."

Paige's heart was pounding so hard it felt as if it would burst out of her chest. She struggled against the plastic confining her wrists. Her bindings were loose, but not loose enough. If she had a little more time, perhaps she could wiggle out of them.

They had to do something. They had to stop her. This woman was insane. She really had planned each last detail, right down to taking over Lydia's life and becoming Molly's mother.

Thank God Lydia had created a will and changed the life insurance policy. If she hadn't, Molly may have gone to live with Abe and Susan. Paige never would've known what this lady had done.

Abe took another step, closing the distance between them. He lifted his hand up to Susan's face, brushing his thumb across her cheekbone. "Tell me you still want that."

Susan's eyes fluttered closed, and Abe made his move. He grabbed for the gun, but Susan sensed his movement. She jerked back, swinging the gun wildly.

Jesse shot up from the floor, and Paige felt a metal object collide against her hand. She grabbed the blade Jesse had slid her way and set to work against her restraints as Jesse darted into the melee. Susan and Abe had toppled to the floor and were wrestling over the weapon. The gun was still in Susan's hand and swung around wildly. Jesse darted back, trying to stay out of the line of accidental fire.

"You can't do this!" Susan screamed. "I've worked too hard!"

The gun went off as Paige's wrists burst free. She staggered to her feet, but her legs were wobbly from sitting so long. Someone let out an awful guttural groan.

Jesse had collapsed to his knees. For one terrible, horrifying moment, as she saw crimson flowing across white concrete, she thought he'd been hit. Her heart felt like it shattered in her chest. She realized then that despite her best efforts not to, she had fallen deeply, irrevocably in love with this man. She couldn't imagine a world without him in it.

Then she realized Abe lay prostrate as Jesse knelt beside him.

Susan began to sob. "Abe!" she cried. "No, no. It wasn't supposed to be this way."

Paige darted forward, plucking up the gun that Susan had forgotten about in her sorrow.

Blood pooled out from Abe, spreading across the

floor. The man's face was wrenched into an expression of pain as he clutched his stomach.

"Help him," Susan moaned. She pressed her hands over her face, tears racing down her cheeks. She looked utterly destroyed.

"I'm trying," Jesse shot back at her. He tore off his flannel shirt, revealing a T-shirt underneath, and pressed it to Abe's wound. He began muttering words of encouragement to Abe.

"Is there a phone in the office?" Paige demanded. Susan didn't respond. She had begun rocking back and forth, moaning and unable to take her gaze off her victim.

Paige pushed to her feet and quickly found a phone to place a call for help. Fortunately, there was a stack of embossed envelopes on the desk. Probably a stack of bills ready to go out. She rattled off the address printed on the corner. The dispatcher asked her to stay on the line, but she disconnected, feeling she would be of more use up front.

Realizing she still had the gun, she opened the chamber and slid the mag out, rendering it useless. She stuffed it into a desk drawer and the ammunition into her pocket. If Susan decided to attack, she'd have to do it without access to a weapon.

She raced back into the warehouse, found the button to open one of the big garage doors and hit it. They were on the edge of town. She was sure she could already hear the distant blaring of sirens.

Hurriedly, she went back to Jesse. His shirt was crimson stained, and Abe's expression had gone slack. Her heart thudded. He couldn't be dead. Though she barely knew the man, he had been a big part of Molly's life. She wanted to make things right with them.

She dropped down next to Jesse. "I called for help. Is there anything else I can do?"

"I just need to slow the bleeding," Jesse said. "That'll give him the best chance for survival."

"Please don't die," Susan moaned from beside them.

Despite herself, Paige actually felt sorry for the woman.

Abe's face had become ashen as blood continued to seep out.

Jesse grabbed her hand with his free one. "I feel like we should pray."

Paige nodded, surprised by his words but agreeing wholeheartedly.

"Please, God," Jesse began, "don't let him die." He turned to Paige. His expression was pained. "I don't know what else to say."

She forced a wobbly smile. "It's enough. God can hear your heart. He knows what we need."

Jesse squeezed her hand as the parking lot flooded with emergency vehicles. Help was finally here. But had it arrived too late?

FOURTEEN

Jesse gripped Paige's hand in his own as they walked up the sidewalk to Abe's home. It had been three days since he'd been shot. Three days since the subsequent arrests of Susan Donnelly, Marcus Cartwright and Charlie Wilkinson.

After hightailing it from Darci's and placing the call to Abe, Charlie had driven to Marcus's house. He knew where Marcus had stashed the down payment from Susan. He'd broken in, intending to grab the cash and leave the state. Law enforcement were staking out the place, waiting for Marcus, and they'd been relieved to capture Charlie instead.

Abe was able to give the address of the new home being built, and Marcus had been apprehended in the middle of digging a shallow grave wide enough for two. The trunk of his car had been full of paraphernalia to assist in abduction. Guns, knives, the Tasers, duct tape, large garbage bags, rags and a bottle of chloroform. The guy had taken the instructions to detain Jesse and Paige at all costs very seriously. The thought sent goose bumps racing down Jesse's spine.

Marcus and Charlie had intended to speak to Darci

that night. She had been bragging to a few too many people about assisting the police. Marcus had wanted to scare her, to get her to keep her mouth shut, but when they'd arrived at her house, they'd recognized Jesse's truck. They'd grabbed the Tasers and waited for Jesse and Paige to come out.

It wasn't until Charlie saw Paige topple to the ground that his conscience got the better of him. He hadn't called Abe entirely out of goodwill. He'd hoped that if Marcus was apprehended, he'd have an easier time taking off with the cash. The night had not turned out the way either Marcus or Charlie had hoped.

"I'm so grateful Abe is going to be all right," Paige said as she rang the doorbell. "I hated thinking he was the one who killed Lydia."

They had explained to Molly that Abe hadn't hurt her mother. They hadn't gone into the whole story. She wasn't old enough for that. She'd held the little beagle in her arms and cried when they told her Abe had been shot, but that he would be okay, that he loved her and would never do anything to hurt her. She would visit with him soon, just not today.

Today, Paige had wanted to see him on her own, because she had a few things to say.

Jesse had insisted on accompanying her. He wanted to support her, but he also found that he wanted to be wherever she was. She would be leaving soon, and he was going to cherish every moment they had left together.

Abe opened the door, and although he was moving slowly, it was clear he was going to survive. The bullet had torn through the fleshy part of his abdomen, missing his organs. It was still a painful flesh wound, and would be for some time, but it could have been so much worse. Paige had called it divine intervention. A week ago, Jesse would've felt inclined to disagree. Now he thought perhaps she was right.

"Come on in." Abe greeted them somewhat hesitantly, even though he'd been forewarned of their arrival. He led them to the living room, where he eased himself into his recliner.

He looked haggard, but at least he was alive. He'd survived losing his wife, being shot and losing his business partner all in the span of a few weeks. No wonder the guy looked rough.

"How are you feeling?" Paige asked.

"Grateful to be alive," Abe said quietly. His lips quivered. "I'm still having a hard time wrapping my head around what Susan did. I knew something was wrong between Lydia and myself. I thought she was spending time with Susan because she needed a friend. I didn't realize that Susan was playing her against me. Lying to her. If only she'd come to me."

He looked pained, and Jesse felt for the guy.

"She didn't come to me either," Paige said sadly. "Lydia was always like that, though. She held things in, tried to do everything on her own."

"Not to mention that Susan was manipulating her," Jesse reminded him.

"I see now why my relationship with Lydia became so tense. I admit, her attitude made me lose my temper more than once. She was distant and irritated. Then there was my gambling problem. I'm embarrassed to say I lost my temper over it more than once." He sighed. "I suppose that played into whatever lies Susan was feeding her, making her afraid of me. It wasn't true, but given the information Lydia had to work with, I see how she came to that conclusion." Tears filled his eyes. "Even though our relationship was rocky, it breaks my heart to know she thought I wanted her dead. It hurts to know her last thought was that I ran her and Molly off the road."

Paige leaned over and squeezed his hand. "She's in a better place now, and I believe she knows the truth."

"Yes, I suppose that's so." He pulled in a shuddering breath. "How is Molly?" he asked. "I realize it's probably too soon, but I'd like to see her. I believe she belongs with you, but I'd still like to be a part of her life. Maybe I can play the role of favorite uncle, since she doesn't have one of those."

Paige nodded. "I think she'd like that."

"You aren't going to pursue custody?" Jesse asked softly.

Abe shook his head. "No. Paige is family. She belongs with Paige."

Jesse wanted to be sure. Paige had been through enough. She didn't need any more unpleasant surprises. "I don't mean to press the issue," Jesse said, "but you did threaten to take Molly away."

Abe frowned. "I was hurt and angry. I guess I was lashing out. Besides, I'm going to have my hands full. I know I need to fight my gambling addiction. And with Susan out of the picture, I'm going to be a very busy man taking complete control of the company. I could never give Molly the time she needs. I know she'll be happy with Paige."

"I hope we can move on from here," Paige said. "I'm sorry I thought you were capable of such an atrocity."

"I was upset and angry at first," Abe admitted, "but now I understand where you were coming from."

"You saved us," Paige said. "Thank you for that."

"I should have called the police," he said apologetically. "But when that man—Charlie, I think you said his name was—when he called, I thought it was a prank. All he said was that the two of you had been taken to my warehouse and something criminal was going on." Abe's brow furrowed. "It just didn't make sense to me. My first instinct was to ignore the call, but in light of what happened to Lydia and that lawyer, I thought I ought to at least check it out. I could barely wrap my head around what I walked in on."

"I never would've gotten out of those bindings if not for you," Jesse admitted.

Abe's lip quirked. "In my line of work, I can't tell you how often that key chain with all of its gadgets has come in handy."

"I hope you don't mind me asking," Jesse said, "but did you know how Susan felt about you?"

Abe looked contemplative for a moment. "I knew she had a crush on me when we were younger," he admitted. "I thought perhaps she still had feelings for me around the time we took over the business. That's why I had hoped to buy her father out. I didn't want there to be any problems. But she met someone and was married shortly after that." He frowned. "She's been married and divorced several times. Profited each time," he admitted. "That's likely where she got the money to pay off those hoodlums," he said. "But no, I had no idea she still felt that way. If I'd known—" he shrugged "—maybe I would've kept Lydia away from her, but I just didn't know."

"There's no point in going there," Paige said. "We can't change the past."

They visited with Abe a bit longer, and by the time they left, Jesse thought Paige seemed lighter, happier, as if an enormous weight had been lifted from her shoulders. He was relieved for her, grateful that the murderer was behind bars, where she couldn't hurt anyone else.

As relieved as he was that Paige and Molly would be safe, his heart was aching over the fact that she would be leaving soon. After this, would he ever see her again? He had already put his feelings for her out there once. It hadn't gone the way he'd hoped, and he didn't know if there was any point in putting himself out there like that again.

Paige looked at her packed suitcase by the front door. She was so grateful for Erin's hospitality. So grateful for Jesse's perseverance and protection. Though she hadn't known them for long, she felt a deep-rooted sense of belonging. They had welcomed her in and treated her and Molly like family. She and Erin had already promised to keep in touch. Grand Junction was only an hour away. She knew Molly would love to return to the ranch every chance she got. And truth be told, so would Paige.

"Are you sure you need to leave today?" Jesse asked, cradling the beagle to his chest.

"You only have a few days of vacation left. You should try to do something enjoyable." She cocked her head to the side. "You are returning to the department, aren't you?"

"Yeah," he said. "I am. I want to help people. I think being a deputy is the best way for me to do that."

"Good," she said. "You are clearly good at what you

do. It's time for you to get back to it. Besides, Molly and I are going to be starting a new life together. Everything has been so chaotic. It's really time we get settled."

Jesse nodded his understanding, but he didn't look happy about it.

She didn't want to leave, but it made no sense to stay. They had already imposed long enough, though Erin had never made them feel that way. Besides, maybe a clean break with Jesse would be for the best. The past three days, he'd been all business. She'd thought about broaching the subject of a relationship, but after declining before, she wondered if she'd pushed him too far away.

She thought of the way Jesse had prayed for Abe. It soothed her heart to see that he was reaching out to the Lord.

Jesse knelt down next to Molly. "I thought you'd want to say goodbye to your little buddy." The puppy squirmed in Jesse's arms, trying to leap into Molly's.

Molly took the puppy, who began to lick her face. Her lips quivered, and tears filled her eyes. Paige's heart ached. She had known Molly was getting too attached to the pup.

"Goodbye, Buddy," Molly said.

Goodbye, Buddy? Paige's eyes widened. She locked gazes with Jesse over Molly's head. The look on his face let her know she hadn't been hearing things. Molly had spoken. She had actually spoken.

Paige struggled for calm. The last thing she wanted to do was make an issue of what had just happened. She didn't want Molly to feel overwhelmed and retreat back into her mode of silence.

"Buddy?" Jesse said softly, his tone so much steadier

than Paige could've managed. "Is that what we're naming this little tyke?"

Molly nodded.

Paige knelt next to them. "That's a good name."

Molly's teary gaze latched on to Paige. "Can we keep her? Please?"

Oh, my. Paige had never heard anything as sweet as her niece's voice. She wasn't sure what to do with the request. She had barely started to wrap her mind around parenting a six-year-old. She couldn't possibly manage a puppy, too. Could she?

One look into her niece's pleading eyes, and she knew she would find a way. She had to. Molly had lost so much, and Buddy had already brought her so much happiness. Paige was sure it was Buddy who had helped her find her voice again. Buddy and Jesse. Their nurturing chats over bottle-feeding and name picking.

She might have to come home on every lunch break. Or maybe ask Mrs. Everly, her elderly neighbor, for help, or even look into doggy day care. Regardless, she would do what she had to do to bring this little ball of love home with them.

"We'll keep her," Paige said. Molly's lips tilted into a smile, and Paige's heart melted a little bit more. She glanced at Jesse. He was blinking hard. Was the man blinking tears away? She knew he'd grown to adore Molly as well.

"She's going to be so happy in her new home," Jesse said.

Molly's lips trembled again.

When Molly threw herself into Jesse's arms, Paige wasn't sure who was more surprised, her or Jesse.

Molly squeezed him tightly. One arm around the little puppy, her other arm around Jesse's neck. "I don't want to go to my new home," Molly said mournfully.

Paige had been so filled with joy when Molly first spoke, but her heart clenched now.

Jesse pressed a kiss onto the top of Molly's head. He looked as crestfallen as her niece.

"You don't want to live with me?" Paige asked, her voice shaky.

Molly slid from Jesse's arms. "I do. But I want to live here, too."

Clearly, the child was torn.

Molly turned to Jesse. "I wish you could come with us. Or I wish we could stay here."

Paige pressed a hand to her stomach. This was not how she had expected their goodbye to go. She knew that Molly liked Jesse, that she felt comfortable with him, but she hadn't realized just how attached her niece had become to the man.

Paige could absolutely relate.

Jesse forced a weak smile. "How would you like to play with Buddy in the tent one last time?"

Molly nodded, scampered off with the puppy and disappeared under the sheet.

Jesse grabbed Paige's elbow. "Can we talk in the den?"

She nodded and let him lead her along to where they could have some semblance of privacy. Her heart pounded. Should she apologize for Molly putting him on the spot like that? It wasn't as if Paige had known she would.

The moment they were in the other room, Jesse spun to face her.

"There's something I need to say to you," he announced.

* * *

Jesse raked a hand through his hair. For the past few days, he'd managed to push Paige's inevitable departure from his thoughts. Kind of. Not completely. Actually, he'd had to make a concerted effort to keep Paige from creeping into his mind.

She was already embedded in his heart.

Paige tilted her head to the side. He should probably make this quick. Molly had spoken, and he was well aware of the significance of that.

"I know you said you need to concentrate on Molly," he began, "and that you won't have time for a relationship, but I'm asking you to reconsider. I have fallen head over heels for that little girl. And quite frankly, for you, too."

There. He'd said it. He'd put himself out there again. He didn't miss the little hitch in her breath, but he wasn't sure what it meant.

"I know you need to devote time to Molly. And you can, but maybe we could devote time to her together."

"Is that what you really want?" she asked.

"More than anything," he said, his voice full of honesty, full of hope and longing.

She looked hesitant, and his heart dipped.

"You're not just saying that because Molly sort of put you on the spot out there?" she asked.

"I'm saying it because I mean it," he replied. He took her hands in his and gently pulled her closer. "I've been on the outs with God for such a long time. I realized I've been quick to blame Him for anything bad that comes my way, but I've never thanked Him for all I've been blessed with. And I *have* been blessed."

Her gaze locked onto his, but she said nothing, as if silently willing him to go on.

"I've had the chance to reflect on my life," he admitted. "And I've realized that all the rocky roads, the twists and the turns, they've all led me to where I am today. Here. With you. I believe I was on that lake for a reason." He'd been angry that God had put Trish into his path only so that she could dupe him, but if not for Trish, he wouldn't have taken time off work. He wouldn't have been at the cabin.

"Ellen is fond of saying that God can work all situations for good, for those who love Him and who are called to His purpose." He squeezed her hands, pulled in a breath and said, "It took me a lot of years to really understand what she was trying to say. I think you and Molly are my purpose. I think you're the reason I was on the lake that day."

He let the words settle between them, let them nestle in and take hold.

A soft smile curved Paige's lips. "Do you really feel that way? That we're God's purpose for your life?"

"I do," Jesse said, meaning it all the way down to his soul. "I think I was meant to protect you and Molly. Not just that day on the lake, not just this past week, but from now on. I've fallen in love with you, Paige. I adore Molly—you know I do." He pressed a hand against his chest. "The thought of losing both of you is almost more than I can bear." He paused, his expression so intense, so full of emotion. "Marry me," he said, almost on a whisper.

Her eyes widened. "What did you say?"

"Marry me," he said, his voice louder and full of conviction. "I know Molly needs to be your focus. But what if she's *our* focus, because we're a family? What do you say?"

Paige pressed a hand over her lips for a moment as she blinked back tears. She nodded, her face breaking into a huge grin. "I say yes! I've fallen in love with you, too. I can't think of anything I want more than for us to be a family. Me, you, Molly."

"Don't forget Buddy!" Molly cried from the doorway. Her grin was as bright as Paige's.

"I would *never*," Jesse said with a laugh.

Cradling Buddy, Molly darted across the room. She leaned her head on Paige's waist and looped an arm around Jesse. She beamed up at him with a smile so radiant it made his heart feel ready to explode with happiness.

He scooped her into his arms and pulled Paige into their hug. Paige laughed and looped her arms around them while Buddy gave slobbery kisses all around.

Their wedding day could not come fast enough, as far as he was concerned. It might not be official yet, but he knew in his heart this was his family. This was where God had led him, and there was nowhere he would rather be.

EPILOGUE

Fifteen months later...

Paige tapped a finger on her chin as she took a quick mental inventory. The bottles had all been sterilized, the cans of formula purchased, and a pile of snuggly blankets had been washed and were waiting. As far as she could tell, they were all set for the three new arrivals they were expecting.

Molly burst into the kitchen, a huge smile lighting up her face. "I just put all of the new toys in a basket." Buddy trotted along behind her, carrying a tug rope, obviously hoping for some playtime.

Paige hoisted an eyebrow. "It'll be a while before the little ones are interested in toys."

"I know," Molly said. "I just want to be ready."

The exuberance in Molly's voice made Paige's heart bubble with happiness. So much had changed this past year. She and Jesse had married at the end of the summer. There hadn't been a librarian job open in Cascade Falls, but Paige was enjoying subbing part-time more than she'd thought she would. She appreciated the change of pace and the extra time to spend with her family.

This spring, they'd purchased a lovely log home on a nice bit of acreage. They were enjoying each other, enjoying Molly and loving the life they were creating together. Molly, of course, missed her mom constantly, but with Paige and Jesse's love and support, she was flourishing.

"I hear them!" Molly cried as the sound of tires crunching on gravel floated through the open window. She darted to the door, Paige only a step behind her. Molly hurried outside, bounded down the steps and nearly flew to where Jesse had parked his truck.

Paige shook her head and smiled as she jogged to catch up.

"The puppies are here!" Molly danced around the truck. Buddy circled her, yipping in excitement, the tug rope dropped along the way and forgotten.

Jesse opened the truck door and glanced at Paige. "Someone is excited."

"Just a little bit," Paige said, her tone wry.

Jesse popped a quick kiss on her cheek, tousled Molly's hair and then opened the back door of his truck. He carefully slid out the crate that housed the three puppies.

"Can I see?" Molly asked as Buddy nosed up close to the crate, trying to get a whiff of the new, tiny foster puppies.

"Let's get them inside first," Jesse suggested.

Paige could hear the tiny little whimpers emanating from the crate. Erin had called them this morning, asking if they'd be interested in taking on the task. The mama dog, a stray, had been hit by a car. The driver had brought her to Erin, who had delivered the babies via C-section, then had worked at setting the mama dog's femur. While Erin felt good about the dog's prognosis, she didn't think she was in any condition to care for her puppies yet.

Hence the phone call pleading for help.

Since Paige and Molly were both on summer vacation, Paige thought it would be a wonderful experience for the two of them. Especially since Molly had benefited so much from helping to care for Buddy. Besides, Paige would be forever grateful to Erin for providing them refuge last year. Taking care of three little pups seemed like a small way to pay Erin back for her kindness.

Once they were inside, Jesse placed the crate on the floor. Molly dropped to her knees, cooing at the wrinkly, squiggly puppies. Paige peeked in as well. They were so itty-bitty, eyes sealed closed, and so very precious.

Molly looked up. Her excitement had slipped into concern. "Is the mama going to be okay?"

"Erin thinks so," Jesse said comfortingly. "She just needs to get some rest."

Molly nodded. Happy with that answer, she became entirely enthralled with the new houseguests.

"We're going to have a lot of middle-of-the-night feedings," Paige said.

"With three pups, we sure will," Jesse agreed.

Paige glanced at Molly, who didn't appear to be paying attention to them in the least.

She leaned in close to Jesse, running her finger along his arm and smiling up into his face. "It'll be good practice."

"Practice for what?" Jesse asked, looking incredulous.

"Sleepless nights." Paige paused and then said, "For when our baby arrives."

"Baby?" he echoed. "What baby?" His eyes widened

as he suddenly caught up with the conversation. "Are you telling me…?"

She nodded, and he whooped, picked her off her feet and twirled her around.

"What?" Molly demanded from her spot on the floor. She eyed them both curiously.

"I'm the happiest person in the world right now," Jesse told her. "That's what."

She tilted her head to the side. "Why?"

"Because I listened to God," he said. He put Paige down and pressed a quick kiss to her forehead. "I followed my heart. If you listen to God, you can never go wrong." His smile was dazzling.

Molly nodded, as if his explanation made perfect sense. They would wait to tell Molly about the little one. She wanted to savor the news with Jesse for a few days, just the two of them.

She glanced around the room, taking in her family. Molly, who was like a daughter to her. Jesse, the husband she now couldn't imagine her life without. Little Buddy, so full of fun and energy. And now, as she pressed a hand to her stomach, a baby on the way.

Jesse's right, Paige thought, her heart swelling with love and gratitude. The events of the past flickered through her mind like a movie on fast-forward. Jesse had said God brought them together. Paige thought so, too. If not for Jesse, she may not have survived the ordeal last year, but He had answered her prayer. Yes, Jesse was absolutely right. *Rely on God. And you can never go wrong.*

* * * * *

Dear Reader,

Thank you for taking the time to join Paige and Jesse on their journey. Jesse had a tough life growing up. His mother was often absent and she had not allowed God to be a part of their lives. Even though that changed when Jesse was taken in by the Coopers, it took many years and some hard situations before he came to understand that God was there for him. That God had always been there for him. He had blamed God for his struggles but hadn't thought to praise God for all he had been blessed with. When Paige comes into his life, he begins to see God acting in miraculous ways.

We all have trials in life. I hope that if you're going through difficult times, you'll lean into God and allow your faith to grow stronger. In these times, it's important to remember all the wondrous things He has done.

I love connecting with my readers. Please join me on my Facebook author page. You can find me at Facebook. com/amitysteffenauthor.

Blessings,
Amity

COMING NEXT MONTH FROM
Love Inspired Suspense

FOLLOWING THE TRAIL
K-9 Search and Rescue • by Lynette Eason
Lacey Jefferson's search for her missing sister quickly turns into a murder investigation, thrusting Lacey and her search-and-rescue dog, Scarlett, into a killer's sights. Now teaming up with her ex-boyfriend, Sheriff Creed Payne, might be the only way to discover the murderer's identity—and survive.

SECRET SABOTAGE
by Terri Reed
Ian Delaney is determined to uncover who sabotaged his helicopter and caused the crash that left him with no memory. But he's convinced his family-appointed bodyguard, Simone Walker, will only get in his way. Can they learn to work together and unravel deadly secrets...before they're hunted down?

SNOWBOUND AMISH SURVIVAL
by Mary Alford
When armed men burst into her patient's house looking for *her*, Amish midwife Hope Christner barely escapes with her pregnant friend. But as the assailants chase them through the woods in a blizzard, Hope's only choice is to turn to Hunter Shetler, the nearest neighbor—and her ex-fiancé.

UNDERCOVER MOUNTAIN PURSUIT
by Sharon Dunn
After witnessing a shooting in a remote location, high-risk photographer Willow Farris races to help—and runs into her old flame, Quentin Decker. Undercover to take down an international smuggler, Quentin has a mission to complete. But to bring the criminals to justice, he and Willow have to get off the mountain alive...

LETHAL CORRUPTION
by Jane M. Choate
Prosecuting a gang leader is the biggest case of deputy district attorney Shannon DeFord's career—if she lives through the trial. With nobody else to trust, Shannon must accept protection from security operative Rafe Zuniga. But when a larger conspiracy is exposed, someone will do anything to keep the truth buried.

COVERT TAKEDOWN
by Kathleen Tailer
With her ex's WITSEC cover blown and someone trying to murder him, it falls to FBI agent Tessa McIntyre to protect the man who left her at the altar. But can she and Gabriel Grayson put their past aside long enough to catch a killer...and ensure they have a chance at a future?

LOOK FOR THESE AND OTHER LOVE INSPIRED BOOKS WHEREVER BOOKS ARE SOLD, INCLUDING MOST BOOKSTORES, SUPERMARKETS, DISCOUNT STORES AND DRUGSTORES.

LISCNM0122A

Get 4 FREE REWARDS!

We'll send you 2 FREE Books plus 2 FREE Mystery Gifts.

Love Inspired Suspense books showcase how courage and optimism unite in stories of faith and love in the face of danger.

FREE Value Over **$20**

SPECIAL EXCERPT FROM

LOVE INSPIRED SUSPENSE
INSPIRATIONAL ROMANCE

Lacey Jefferson's search for her missing sister quickly turns into a murder investigation, thrusting Lacey and her search-and-rescue dog, Scarlett, into a killer's sights. Now teaming up with her ex-boyfriend, Sheriff Creed Payne, might be the only way to discover the murderer's identity—and survive.

Read on for a sneak peek of
Following the Trail *by Lynette Eason,*
available February 2022 from Love Inspired Suspense.

Had he really just offered employment to the woman who'd broken his heart? There was no way he wanted to be stuck working with her day in and day out, a constant reminder of how she'd chosen the big city over him—over them. Then again, she could accuse him of doing the same thing to her.

But that was different. This was his home.

And hers, too, whether she wanted to admit it or not.

"Seriously," he found himself saying, "it would be full-time with benefits and everything."

"As what, Creed?"

"A deputy. And leader of the K-9 unit."

"You don't have a K-9 unit."

"We would if you started one."

She gaped at him. "I need to talk to you about Fawn, but first I have something I need to take care of."

"What?"

"Scarlett was real antsy around that fallen tree trunk," she said. "I want to go take a look at what she was reacting so strongly to."

Creed nodded. "I'll go out there with you, and we can talk on the way."

Lacey studied him for a moment, then gave a short dip of her head. "Can you keep Regina and the others here until we finish checking out that tree trunk?" she asked.

He narrowed his eyes. "Why? Don't tell me Scarlett is trained in cadaver search, as well."

Lacey shook her head. "She started out that way but hated it and was terrible at it. She apparently just really did not like the smell and would be very skittish when she got close to a dead body."

"Can't say I blame her," he muttered.

"And she would sneeze. She was acting that way out by the tree."

Creed froze. "I see. And you think there's a dead body out there?"

"I don't think so, I'm…afraid so."

Don't miss
Following the Trail *by Lynette Eason,*
available February 2022 wherever
Love Inspired Suspense books and ebooks are sold.

LoveInspired.com

LISEXP0122-A